BOWLING BODIES AT SPARE LANES ALLEY

⁂

LAURA HERN

Copyright © 2023 by Laura Hern

All rights reserved.

No part of this publication may be reproduced, stored in a retrieval system or transmitted in any form or by any means, without the prior permission in writing of the publisher and/or the copyright owner nor to be otherwise circulated in any form of binding or cover other than that in which it is published without a similar condition, including this condition, being imposed on the subsequent purchaser.

All the characters in this book are fictitious, and any resemblance to actual persons living or dead is purely coincidental.

Cover Design/Interior Design: Linda Boulanger

ISBN: 978-1-61752-229-1

Contents

Thank You	v
Social Media	vii
Reviews - You Can Make A Difference	ix
Praise for the Author	xi
Introduction	xiii
Chapter 1	1
Chapter 2	14
Chapter 3	29
Chapter 4	43
Chapter 5	57
Chapter 6	72
Chapter 7	86
Chapter 8	101
Chapter 9	117
Chapter 10	127
Chapter 11	143
Chapter 12	159
Murder in the Backwater Preview	165
Christmas Corpse at Caribou Cabin Preview	179
About the Author	193
Also by Laura Hern	195

Thank You

Thank you for supporting all authors by buying, reading, and reviewing books. I give you my utmost gratitude! I couldn't continue to tell stories if it weren't for you and for the support team that surrounds me!

Social Media

Laura Hern Social
Website & Newsletter:
https://www.laurahern.com

Facebook:
https://www.facebook.com/laurahernauthor

BookBub:
bookbub.com/authors/laura-hern

Also in series:
The Family Tree Murders
Murder In The Backwater
Curtain Call At Brooksey's Playhouse
Christmas Corpse At Caribou Cabin
And more coming soon!

Reviews - You Can Make A Difference

If you've enjoy my book, please leave a review!
Bowling Bodies at Spare Lanes Alley

Reviews are the most important and powerful ways to spread the word about my books.

I believe there is something even more effective and personal than any type of ad.

It's you! Building a relationship with committed and loyal readers is powerful!

An honest review will help bring my books to other readers, something no amount of advertising can accomplish!

I humbly and gratefully ask you to spend a few minutes leaving a review if you enjoyed my book. It can be as short or long as you like.

Thank you and blessings on your day! Laura Hern

Praise for the Author

"Fabulous"
"Laura Hern writes easy, enjoyable reads that will make you laugh out loud. Extremely well written and the characters are simply a hoot!"
Terry

"Fun easy read with suspense and unexpected twists"
"I am now a Laura Hern fan. She writes plot twists that are exciting and the suspense will keep you wanting more all the way through the book. The best part was feeling like a part of this group of friends."
T. K.

Introduction

"What crazy weather! I've been running all over town in this icy rain!" Della shivered as she hurried through the door of Babe's House of Caffeine and toward the Whoopee's regular table.

"Mother Nature must think it's March, not October." Francy grinned and pulled out the chair between her and Lainey. "Sit down and dry out. Mom's running a bit late, too."

"Are you still trying to figure out a costume for the bowling fundraiser?" Lainey asked. "I think I've decided on mine!"

"Didn't Francy tell you? We're going as the Blues Brothers!" I'm Jake and she's Elwood." She leaned closer to Lainey and, looking at Francy, pretended to whisper. "She's jealous of my dancing abilities!"

"Absolutely not!" Francy smirked. "I have dance

moves that make Elwood look like a beginner!" She stood up, pushed her chair from the table, and began stomping her feet, shaking, and wiggling her body, waving her hands in the air while shouting 'Hallelujah'!

Everyone in the cafe laughed. Some clapped and chanted, "Go Francy. Go Francy. Go Francy."

"Okay, okay! You *can* dance, but I'm still the lead singer," Della chuckled.

Francy stopped, turned to the cafe patrons, and took a bow while they applauded. She pretended to blow kisses to thank them, then turned to sit down at the table again.

"Whew! That's hard work. I should have done more of Mom's 'Sweating to the Oldies' workout videos!" she said breathlessly. "I'm going to need a large Caramel Macchiato."

"Maybe you need something skinny instead…like water?" Vera laughed. She had walked into the cafe unnoticed while Francy was showing off her talents. "I've seen no one move their body quite like that…and I saw the original Blues Brothers!" She walked over to Francy and patted her on the back.

"Thanks for the vote of confidence, Mom." Francy shook her head, then smiled. "I remember watching you and Dad dancing in the front room. What was that Beach Boys' song?"

"It was Surfin' USA. Your Dad could shake a leg! And we were pretty darn good, if I say so myself!"

The Whoopee group were regulars at Babe's, and Maliea, their favorite server, brought their usual drink orders to their table.

"Are you taking part in the bowling tourney this weekend at Spare Lanes Alley? I heard rumors that Shep's old team is getting together again. Is that right?" Maliea asked. "My hubby and I have been practicing. His men's team went to the US Open Championships in Reno this past Spring."

"Wow! They must be good bowlers," Lainey replied. "The four of us are a team. We're calling ourselves the Whoopee Pin Slayers."

"Vera liked the name Whoopee Lickity-Splitters," Della frowned, rolling her eyes.

"It was only a suggestion," Vera muttered back. "Better than Shep's idea of the Whoopee Gutter Gals."

Maliea laughed loudly. "I think the Pin Slayers sounds like a team to be reckoned with!" She smiled. "I've got to get back to work. Good luck and see you next weekend."

The ladies sipped their drinks and talked more about their team's name and costumes. Vera looked toward the door to see Shep Morton entering the cafe. He walked over, gave her a quick peck on the cheek, and said hello to the others.

"I thought you were grocery shopping for the Backwater restaurant? Did you finish early?" Vera asked as he grabbed a chair from an adjacent table and sat next to her.

"I took the food to the restaurant and put Ryan to work cooking tonight's menu specials. It's been great having him to train. He's going to be an excellent chef one day."

"What is his last name again?" Della asked. "Bullock or Bicklum or…"

"It's Ballulah. Ryan Ballulah. He's Charlie Crowfoot's nephew and the Hayward's son-in-law."

"I'm curious, Shep," Lainey began. "Vera says you are getting your old bowling buddies together for the tourney this weekend. Have you and Charlie mended your differences?"

"Well, not exactly, but since I hired Ryan, Charlie agreed to bowl with our team…only to help the Hayward's out."

"I was sad to learn about Gerry and Phoebe. Wonder if this fundraiser will be enough to help them." Francy said.

"Isn't a famous bowler coming to the fundraiser? Was it Pete Weber?" Della asked.

Shep shook his head no and shrugged his shoulders. "I heard rumors about that but understand he couldn't make it. Not sure who, if anyone, might attend from the PBA. It's been a long time since Gerry was an active member."

"Paul had lunch with Dan Evans from the bank last

week. He mentioned the only thing that could help the Haywards is a miracle."

The group fell silent for a moment, all deep in their own thoughts. Vera took hold of Shep's hand and, with a tearful voice, was the first to speak.

"All kinds of miracles happen every day." She looked at Shep and squeezed his hand. "How you react or don't react to that miracle is another thing entirely."

Lainey nodded and thought to herself, *can miracles erase years of lies, deception, and the possibility of murder?*

Chapter One

Mirror Falls was reluctantly accepting that summer had ended, and the hustle and bustle of tourists had finished for the year, leaving an emptiness behind. It's a time when children go back to school, parents put away boats, golf clubs, and motorcycles, and the pace of everyday life slows down a bit. But for a few people, it is a time of excitement and expectation of the weekly night meetings with friends and foes over the coming eight months. It's bowling season!

From Labor Day through the first weeks in April, bowling alleys everywhere come alive with sounds of heavy bowling balls being tossed or rolled down an oily lane and crashing into ten hour-glass shaped pins. The sounds of cheers for strikes, high-fives for spares, and groans when the ball misses its target grow louder and softer like the tide rolling in and out. The smell of greasy fries, burgers, pizza, and old sweaty bowling shoes is as welcoming as the hot apple pie at grandma's house. They've waited months for the opening of the season.

Since the days of the ancient Egyptians, people have thrown a ball at pins trying to outscore their peers. It's not just for enjoyment. It's a competition and the stakes can be very high. Spare Lanes Alley, built in the 1960's, was the only bowling alley within a thirty-mile radius of Mirror Falls. It had been closed for many years and was in need of repair when Gerald and Phoebe Hayward bought it.

The couple invested their savings and spent a few years refurbishing and renovating the twenty-lane facility. And for a while, it was a popular meeting place for all ages. From birthday parties and leagues every night to Scotch Doubles tournaments on weekends, Spare Lanes was *the* hot spot where local celebrity bowlers and newbie bowlers gathered.

When the pandemic hit and daily life came to a standstill, Spare Lanes closed its doors once more. Gerry and Pheebs, as the Haywards were fondly called, had a difficult time making ends meet. Unknown to his wife, Gerry had put a second mortgage on their home to keep from losing the bowling alley. After two years, the beloved king and queen of the local bowling community were facing foreclosure on both properties.

For many years prior, an area association of churches called Aaron's Hands had helped hundreds of families by sponsoring various fundraising events. Pastor Leon Keegler from the First Methodist Church, an avid bowler himself and the association board chair, volunteered to oversee the Hayward's fundraiser. Members posted flyers everywhere possible within a hundred-mile radius of Mirror Falls. A Twin Cities news reporter interviewed him to drum up more media attention. A television interview aired on a regular Thursday Whoopee card night, and the ladies listened, laughed, and decided it would be fun to take part in the event.

Since then, they had been diligently working on their costumes and had met Shep at Babe's to compare notes.

"What prompted Pastor Keegler to name it the Holy Rollers Bowling Tournament?" Francy laughed, looking at her friends around the table. "That's a perfect name!"

"It sounds like so much fun," Della replied. "Dressing up as your favorite character and bowling at midnight under black lights is a terrific idea!"

Vera grinned. "I remember your dad's team never

missed the Midnight Madness Bowling one Saturday night a month. Each person paid for three games of bowling. There were black lights, disco type music, bowling pins that glowed in the dark and tons of prizes. Every lane was full, and there was usually a waiting list."

"Didn't he win a set of Star Wars coffee mugs?" Francy asked. "Seems like he was always winning a prize of some sort."

"The glasses featured a picture of Fred Flintstone throwing a rock bowling ball. I still have them packed away somewhere. He won the strangest things. Once he came home with a plastic trophy of a big old turkey." Vera shook her head.

"I dusted that thing so many times. He finally told me that a turkey in bowling meant you had three strikes in a row. Dad took me bowling a few times, but I never quite got the hang of throwing a curve ball like he did."

Vera laughed loudly. "But you could sure surf that gutter all the way down the lanes!"

"Hey, Lainey, didn't you say that you were a bowler at one time?" Della asked. "Maybe you can be the ringer on our team."

"I'm no ringer," Lainey chuckled. "I bowled a couple of seasons and I think my average was a whopping 134. But I am looking forward to playing again."

"What costume did you come up with?" Della looked at Francy. "We think you'd make a great Inspector Gadget!" The two of them chuckled.

"Nope. I'm going as Spock." She raised her right hand, created a letter V with her fingers and said, "Live long and prosper."

"Mom won't tell me what her costume is," Francy added. "Neither will Shep."

"It's a surprise," Vera answered. "We're going to enter the best costume contest and want to make sure no one else comes as our characters." She sipped on her coffee before continuing. "Shep thinks we need to practice on the lanes. He's willing to come and give us pointers. He reserved two lanes for us this evening."

Francy looked at Della and Lainey and gave them a slight wink. "Mom, it's for fun. Do you really think we need to practice?"

"It's just a suggestion," Shep chimed in. "Lanes can be sticky and you may need to pick out a bowling ball or two. And it's a good idea to see how those great rented bowling shoes feel on your feet." He was grinning from ear to ear.

"So…" Lainey smiled and put her elbows on the table looking directly into his eyes, "you're saying we *need* practice?"

Shep kept her gaze for a long moment. Neither blinked. "As a member of the Professional Bowlers

Association and team captain of the reigning area bowling team champs, The Pocket Pounders," he rubbed his hand across his chin and then grinned. "Yes. You need to practice!"

Everyone laughed and, after finishing their coffees, agreed to meet at Spare Lanes Alley at 5 p.m. that evening. They waved goodbye and each left the cafe. As Lainey was driving home, she wondered where her old bowling bag and shoes might be. She wasn't looking forward to wearing rented bowling shoes. "I wonder if they are in the attic?" she said aloud as she pulled into her garage. She got out of the car, pulled down the attic ladder, and climbed up into the small space.

Luckily, it was still daylight, and she could see several storage tubs stacked in rows. She walked slowly, trying to read the faded black magic marker labeling she had put on the lids of the tubs. Sure enough, packed in a plastic tub toward the back of the attic, was her grey and purple bowling bag. She removed the lid and took out the bag. The two handles on top were loose, but she made it down the attic ladder before one of them gave way.

"Crime-a-nellie," she said, walking into the house. "I don't remember the ball being this heavy." She set the bag on her kitchen countertop and unzipped it. There, in all its dusty, sparkly glory, was her 12-pound bowling ball, the Purple Hammer. A family friend ran the bowling alley where she grew up and had talked her into buying a Hammer many years ago. He said it would force the ball to hook into the pocket and all the pros were using them. He measured her hand and drilled the thumb and finger holes exactly to fit her. And to her surprise, he had engraved the words "Lainey's Purple Hammer" on it.

She took the Hammer out of the bag and placed it on a chair next to her. She looked inside the bag noticed her old shoes had been squished flat underneath the weight of the ball. Lainey reached inside to retrieve the shoes. They were hard and stiff.

"Hmm," she muttered as she laid them on the countertop. "It looks like rented shoes for me this time around." Turning her attention back to the bag, she saw several score cards, weekly league reports, and an old hand towel she used to clean the oil off her ball. *These bring back wonderful memories*. She looked at the old records and smiled.

The rest of the afternoon passed quickly as she answered a few work emails. She noticed it was getting close to 4 o'clock. Lainey shut down her computer, walked over to pick up the now clean grey and purple bowling bag with the freshly duct-taped handles and headed to her car. She set the bag on the front passenger seat and turned on classic radio station 148 to finish listening to an episode of 'Yours, Truly, Johnny Dollar' that she had started earlier that day. She pulled into the parking lot of the bowling alley about the same time as Della and Francy.

"I hope people turn out for the fundraiser this weekend," Lainey said as the friends walked toward the alley's main entrance.

"Gerry and Pheebs made many friends over the years," Della answered.

"Let's hope for more friends than enemies," Francy said quietly.

They opened the double glass doors and walked inside. There were a few lanes with bowlers, but most lanes were empty. One family was having a child's birthday party, complete with cake, streamers, and balloons. Fifteen first graders were giggling, sliding on the slick floor in their socked feet, and trying to throw balls bigger than themselves down lane number 5.

Shep and Vera were standing at the check-in counter, talking with the young man working behind the cash register. The ladies walked up to sign in.

"Girls, let me introduce you to an up-and-coming PBA star, Chad Devon," Shep said. "He's been helping the Hayward's out here in the evenings." He turned to Chad and winked. "This is the famous, or should I say infamous, Whoopee group that Vera's been telling you about!" He grinned and introduced each one. Chad put his hand out to shake each of the ladies' hands.

"I've been hearing about your group." Chad's smile exposed the cutest dimples on either side of his mouth.

"I understand you are quite the celebrities around Mirror Falls. You have a table at Babe's House of Caffeine named in your honor, correct?"

Lainey felt her cheeks turn red. "It's not named the Whoopee table, but we meet there regularly." She winked at Della and Francy, as if to signal them to say something.

"Didn't I read something in the paper, Chad, that you entered the singles competition at last year's open bowling championship in Vegas?" Della asked, trying to change the subject. "My husband said it's difficult to get on the PBA tour."

"Let's just say for the past three years, I've been bowling full time. I've taken part in the tour qualifying rounds, trying to earn exemptions to get me into the elite PBA events." He took a big breath. "It's a grueling journey and harder to make the tour than you think."

"How did you become interested in making bowling your career choice?" Francy asked. "I've heard that it's hard to make a lot of income unless you are one of those elite bowlers."

"Yes, Ma'am," the young man answered. "My family has been involved in bowling since before the days of prohibition. My great grandfather helped build the bowling alley in the basement of St. Pete's in the Twin Cities. Maybe I have the bowling gene in my blood."

"I've read about those underground bowling alleys built in church basements," Lainey added. "I think very few of those remain, and St. Pete's was still in use until a few years ago."

"That's right," Chad replied. "Men used to meet in those secret church basements to gamble, drink, and smoke." He paused, then said, "Now, who needs shoes? I've got you on lanes 17 and 18."

Each took their shoes and walked over to their assigned lanes. Shep was busy entering their names into the automatic scoring system while the ladies got ready to bowl. The lanes were primed and the rack of pins at the end of the alley stood proudly, teasing the next bowler to knock them over.

"Well, well," a familiar voice began. "Shep told me you might practice this evening. It's good to see you all." Gerry Hayward was walking toward them from the back of the alley. He had been working on the pin setting machines on a couple of lanes.

"Hello, Gerry!" Shep stood up and walked over to meet him. "Still having trouble with the pin setter on 8 and 9?"

"Yea, these old machines can be cranky." He wiped his hands on a red cleaning rag he pulled from his back pocket and shook hands. "Giving the gals some pointers tonight?" He smiled at the ladies. "Or are they giving you pointers?"

"We're going to win the tournament this weekend," Vera replied. "And wait till you see…"

"Sorry to interrupt you," Chad said loudly as he

hurriedly walked toward them. "I found this envelope under the cash register drawer. It says 'Gerry...Urgent'. I thought you better see it now," he said, handing it to Gerry.

"What? This was in the cash drawer?" he asked with a puzzled look on his face. Turning the envelope from front to back, he tore open one end. As he pulled out the paper from inside, something dropped onto the floor. Lainey walked over to pick it up. It was a faded newspaper article clipping.

"This is one of the old scorecards we used before we had the new digital system," Gerry commented. "It's for a full game, but the fourth frame has been outlined with a yellow highlighter. The letters CC are in the area where the first ball pin count would be, and the letters PH are in the box where a spare count would be."

"This fell out when you opened the envelope," Lainey said, handing the clipping to him. "It looks like an old bowling alley. I think it's a copy of some old newspaper article. Look closely at the men in the photo. It's got to be from the 1920's or 30's."

Gerry looked at the photo, then back at the scorecard. He shrugged his shoulders and passed the two items to Shep. Then he turned toward Chad.

"Did you see who put this in the cashbox?" he questioned the young man.

"I have no idea. No one's been near the register since I came to work tonight."

"I think you're right, Lainey," Shep said as he handed her both items. "It's not a clear copy, but certainly looks like how men dressed back then."

"Hmm. Wonder what the scorecard has to do with this article? Della, how would you feel about doing research on this article? Have you got time?"

"I always have time for history!" she replied, taking the photo and scorecard from Lainey. "Gerry, do you mind if I take these home for a few days?"

"You're more than welcome to. It means nothing at all to me."

"Ahem…" Vera pretended to clear her throat. "I have this lovely blue ball that is begging to be thrown at some pins. Can we practice now?"

"Sure, Sweetie," Shep winked at Francy. "The lane is all yours."

"Give me a second. I have to stretch."

What followed was an awkward sequence of movements that made the group bite their lips to keep from laughing. Vera rolled her shoulders a few times while moving her head in a circle. She spread her feet apart, took a few deep breaths, exhaling each time with a squeaky grunting sound. Then, bending over as if to touch her toes, a long popping sound filled the air.

Vera stood straight up, eyes and mouth wide open as if she had seen a ghost. She recovered quickly and, pretending nothing had happened, she took her hand and waved it across her nose to clear the air. She looked at her friends and pointed to Shep.

"I've heard that you always bet on the dog that poops just before the race. Now you can place your bets!"

Chapter Two

The Whoopee Pin Slayers spent the next couple of hours bowling, laughing, and consuming two orders of the kitchen's finest fried cheese curds. As they were packing up their things, Francy, noticing Phoebe Hayward standing behind the cash register, walked over to talk with her. It surprised her to see dark circles around her friend's eyes.

"Pheebs! Good to see you. Are you working tonight?"

"Not exactly. Just closing out the register to balance our books." There was a definite strain in her voice and a look of weariness on her face. "Have you seen Chad this evening?"

"He was here earlier, and so was Gerry. Why?"

Pheebs let out a soft sigh and tried to smile. "Oh, no

special reason. Getting ready for the tournament on Saturday?"

The two talked for a couple of minutes until Lainey and Della were ready to leave. They said goodbye to Pheebs and walked outside to their cars. It was then that Francy stopped and questioned her friends.

"Did you think Pheebs looked okay? I mean, did you see those dark circles under her eyes?"

"I thought she looked tired," Della replied. "The stress of losing not only your home and your business, but all of your savings, has to have taken a toll on her."

"I agree with you. But I feel like something else is bothering her. She asked me if I had seen Chad this evening. Wouldn't she know if he was working?" Lainey asked. She had first felt a familiar tingling in her stomach when she looked at the items Gerry had received in the envelope. After seeing Pheebs, she knew her intuition was alerting her once again.

"There is definitely something else going on," Della said. "I'm eager to do research on that newspaper article. It's very odd that the envelope appeared, and Chad disappeared."

"Let me know what you find," Lainey answered. "I'm working at home tomorrow."

Della nodded. "Will do."

"Hey, Lainey, did you leave your bowling bag in the alley?" Francy asked. "Want me to get it for you?"

"Shep has a locker at the alley, and he let me keep it there until Saturday's tournament."

"By the way, you handled that purple thunder well! Your best game was a 145, right?"

Lainey chuckled. "It's a purple Hammer, Francy. And yes, I had a good night!"

The friends said goodbye, got into their cars, and drove away. The radio classics channel was playing in Lainey's car, but she wasn't listening as she drove home. Questions were swirling in her mind. How did someone put the envelope in the cash register with no one noticing and who did it? Why was Gerry not concerned about it? Why had Chad found the envelope precisely when Gerry was in the building? Why was Pheebs' worried about the cash register closing tonight? Chad had closed out many times in the past, right?

Those questions and more kept Lainey's mind churning all night. She tossed and turned, unable to sleep. By 3 a.m., she stopped fighting sleep, got up, dressed, and sat down at her computer. Her cat, Powie, followed her, stretching his legs before jumping in her lap. He gave her a disgusted look that she had disturbed his sleep.

"Don't give me that look," she told him, stroking his head. "At least you can go back to sleep. I have work to do."

The black cat purred for a short time, closed his

eyes, and was out like a light. Lainey turned on her computer and began catching up on emails and reports. It was almost 9 o'clock when someone rang the doorbell. She walked to the front door wondering who it was. She hadn't ordered anything lately that required delivery.

When Lainey had moved into her house, the front door did not have a screen door in front of it. She had gone down to the local home improvement store and purchased a glass door. After her husband had died, she felt safer having an extra barrier between her and whoever was standing on her porch.

It surprised her to see Bailee Hayward Ballulah standing in front of the glass door. She opened the door and greeted the young lady.

"Good morning, Bailee. Come on in here," she said. "How's married life treating you?"

The newlywed smiled, walked inside, and started to take off her shoes.

"You don't need to take off your shoes," Lainey smiled. "Let's sit down in the kitchen. How about a cup of coffee?"

"No, thanks. I can't stay very long," Bailee answered. "We've been married for almost eight months now. Ryan has been working for Shep Morton at the Backwater restaurant and I've been busy with my job at the newspaper office. Two weeks ago, I was promoted to the feature community events reporter."

"That's terrific! I'm sure you'll do a fantastic job covering Mirror Falls."

"Thanks. I know you're wondering why I'm here." Taking off the backpack she was wearing, she unzipped it, pulled out a large manilla envelope and handed it to Lainey. "Last night, when I was leaving work, I found this taped to my car windshield. I have said nothing to Ryan about it, and I'm hoping you can help me."

Lainey opened the envelope and took out the two items inside. Her eyes narrowed and the tingling sensation in her stomach returned with a vengeance. She was holding a large feather that had red paint splattered on it...and a bowling scorecard with frame 4 highlighted. Like the one Gerry had received the night before, the frame had initials in it. BB was in the pin count area and GH was in the spare count area.

Bailee saw the concern and confusion on Lainey's face. "I don't know who left this or why. Did you know that Ryan's family is Ojibwe Tribe?"

"I knew he was Charlie Crowfoot's nephew. Do you think that has something to do with the feather?"

"Ryan's family has a very proud heritage. They attend annual Pow Wows, dressing in their native regalia."

"A Pow Wow is a celebration of American Indian culture, correct?"

"Oh yes! It's a time of celebration: dancing, singing, and honoring ancestors. I've attended two of them. I brought a photo of Ryan in his feathered headdress." She opened the backpack again and handed a photo to Lainey. "It's beautiful, isn't it?"

Lainey looked at the photo for a long moment before handing it back to Bailee.

"I'm sure you noticed this feather is similar to the ones in the photo."

"I recognized it immediately." Bailee hesitated. "While Ryan was working last evening, I checked his closet. This feather is identical to the ones in his headdress. I do not know why some bowling scorecard was in the envelope, either. I'm a bowler, but Ryan isn't."

Lainey thought hard about whether she should mention the scorecard that Gerry had gotten last night. She needed more information and didn't want to cause further worry to the young bride.

"What exactly do you want me to do?" she asked Bailee. "I agree that something strange is going on here."

"You have much more experience in investigations than I do…" her voice trailed off and a sadness filled the air. "Mom and Dad are going through so much right now and, while I appreciate the fundraiser, the offers of help from their friends and the media attention are embarrassing." She shook her head, trying to stop her eyes from tearing. "That sounded terrible," she apologized. "What I meant was…"

Lainey put her hand on Bailee's shoulder. "You don't need to explain anything. It's a difficult situation and you love your parents. Your friends understand that."

"While I was in school, Dad was still in the PBA, and I was so proud of him. I'd take one of his bowling trophies or his latest award patch to show and tell. He even spoke to my class on career day, encouraging them to become bowlers."

"I understand he worked his way up to a Regional Manager position. That's difficult to do."

Bailee took a deep breath and let it out. The frown on her face betrayed her true feelings.

"I was in grade school when the PBA filed charges against him and didn't fully realize the impact it had on our family's future." She raised her right hand and brushed through her short brown hair. "In college, I researched the incident and, to be honest, I'm still mad at Dad about it to this day. He and Mom never mentioned the matter to me. Now, the entire community knows that Dad still has a gambling issue. It's common knowledge that he mortgaged both their house and the bowling alley to cover his debts. That's the reason Pastor Keegler organized this fundraiser." She paused once more. "All the harsh and ugly feelings I tried to put to rest have come back to haunt me."

The two fell silent, each waiting for the other to speak. Lainey's mind was racing with thoughts of how

Gerry's past played a part in these surprise envelopes. But who was sending these, and why now? What does an Indian feather have in common with a newspaper clipping?

"I'm here to ask you to help me find out why someone gave me these. I'm too close to the entire situation to be objective about it."

"Of course, I'll help you. Can you get me access to old newspaper records? In my college days, they stored old articles on microfiche. I'm guessing there are digital copies now?"

Bailee laughed aloud. "One of my textbooks talked about microfiche! Reading those old films must have been like working in the dark ages!"

"Now that makes me feel ancient," Lainey grinned.

"No offense," she answered, still giggling. "I have access to articles, depending on how old they are. What are you looking for?"

"I'm not sure, but would it bother you if you gave me more information about what happened with your dad and the PBA? I realize it's not pleasant for you, but any articles pertaining to that might give us more clues."

"I figured you would ask for that. Yes, I'll get all I can for you. What else?"

"I'm wondering where you can get feathers like the one in the envelope. Is that something you buy in a store or is it a special-order item? Can you find out?"

"You bet. While I love Ryan, his family hasn't embraced me as I had hoped. But I'll do some checking and see what I can find."

"Great. I'd like to keep the feather and the scorecard for a while." Lainey carefully put them back into the manilla envelope. "I saw your mom last night at the bowling alley. How is she holding up?"

"She puts on a brave face, but I overheard them arguing a few days ago. She told Dad her entire married life had been trying to clean up the messes he'd created. Mom said she hated him for it. I can see why she feels angry."

Lainey nodded. "It hasn't been easy for any of you. Let's pray that the fundraiser will be a tremendous success."

Bailee gave Lainey a big hug, zipped up her backpack, and headed to the front door. Lainey's cell phone rang as she closed the door. She locked the door and hurried to her office desk to answer the phone before the caller hung up. The caller ID showed it was Della.

"Morning," Lainey answered. "You're up early."

"I almost hung up. Usually, you answer on the first or second ring," she replied. "And it's close to noon, I'll have you know!"

"You're right," she looked at her watch, not realizing Bailee's visit had taken so long. "Have you got any information on the bowling picture article?"

"Yes, I do. Want to come to my place? I think you'd better see what I found as soon as possible."

"How about you come here? I'll make some tuna salad sandwiches for us. Sound good?"

"Whoop! My favorite! Hope you have boiled eggs to put in it," a familiar voice shouted over the phone.

"Francy? You're at Della's? You two have been busy today."

"She barged in here about eight this morning," Della said curtly. "Now that's early, according to my time standards!"

"Wait just a minute. I came armed with a caramel macchiato *and* a piece of cinnamon coffee cafe for your breakfast."

Lainey laughed. "Okay, okay, you two. Bring everything you have found and come over. Yes, Francy, I'll put boiled eggs in the salad."

"And purple onions?" Della asked gingerly. "I love purple onions."

"If I have one, I'll add it," Lainey sighed, rolling her eyes. "Anything else you want to put in the tuna salad?" She heard her two friends laugh.

"Once you see the information we have, I think you'll need to make double chocolate brownies, too." Francy kidded. "We'll be there in half an hour."

Lainey ended the call, walked into the kitchen, moved the manilla envelope Bailee had given her from the countertop to the dining room table, then began preparing lunch. By the time her friends rang the doorbell, the meal was ready. Lainey opened the door and welcomed them in.

"As instructed, your tuna salad awaits you. Please, come in. Sit down and prepare to enjoy a scrumptious lunch." She pretended to bow, putting out her arm to point the way to the kitchen bar. The friends giggled, walked inside, and sat down. They talked while they ate.

"What have you found about the newspaper article?" Lainey asked. "Were you able to narrow it down to a certain day or time?"

"Actually, it's a fairly famous photo," Della said as she took several printed pages out of her purse. "Or at least it's well known around this area." She handed the papers to Lainey.

"It was taken in 1928, in the basement bowling alley of The Church of the Ascension," Francy stated. "The men, well-known bootleggers, met there to drink."

"I see. Prohibition didn't end till 1933, I think. Selling liquor was still illegal," Lainey commented. "I'm not familiar with that church, though. Where is it located?"

"It was torn down in the early 60's and the Mirror Falls Mall for All Seasons was built in its place," Francy answered. "The city renamed it Center Point Mall in the 80's."

"You said the men in the photo were bootleggers?

Did you find any names? And why was their picture in the newspaper when it was supposed to be a secret meeting place?"

Della swallowed a bite of tuna salad and took a drink of ice water before she answered.

"The photo was taken by a reporter pretending to be a bootlegger. He was spying for the police, giving them information to bust rings around the area. The copy Gerry got last night was just a small portion of the entire article."

And get this," Francy added. "One man was killed in the raid. Della is going to search more to find out his name. But the reporter's name was Phineas Hayward."

Lainey leaned forward in her chair in surprise. "Hayward as in related to Gerry Hayward?"

Francy folded her arms and flashed a huge grin. "Yep. It's Gerry's grandfather."

"Phineas Hayward," Lainey said under her breath. "Della, let me see that scorecard again."

"Great minds think alike, my friend," Della added as she handed the paper to Lainey. "Two of the letters in frame 4 are PH."

The friends looked from one to another, nodding and smiling. Even though the letters PH had the same initials as Phineas Hayward, Lainey knew not to count her chickens before they hatched. She needed more information before she would be convinced the two were the same person. But her mind was already churning with fresh ideas, especially since finding out there was a second scorecard with initials on it. She put down the paper, got up, and walked over to the dining room table. She picked up the manilla envelope and walked back to her seat.

"Before we get ahead of ourselves," Lainey began, holding up the envelope she had gotten earlier. "I had a visitor this morning."

Lainey opened the envelope and placed the feather and scorecard on the table in front of her friends. They took turns examining them while she told them of Bailee's visit. She explained about Ryan's family heritage and about the headdress he had with the same type of feathers in it.

"Bailee opened up that she still feels anger over the PBA incident with Gerry," Lainey said. "I guess she was pretty embarrassed as a kid when it all went down."

"I remember Mom talking about that," Francy commented. "Shep and my dad were very involved with the PBA at the time, too. Dad said they charged Gerry with betting on bowling tournaments and trying to influence bowlers to lose deliberately.

"I'm surprised they didn't send him to prison," Della commented.

"It's my understanding that the PBA took into consideration his family and his years of service with the organization. Gerry's lawyer plea bargained, and instead of a prison term, the PBA banned him from participating or being a member of any PBA organization for life." Francy finished. "Mom said the local papers and news channels carried the story for weeks. I'm sure it had to be embarrassing for Pheebs, too."

"Bailee also mentioned that she overheard her mom and dad arguing. She said her mom told him she hated him," Lainey shrugged. "I'm not sure why, but these two envelopes appear to be attempts to harass the Haywards. Bailee is going to look up some old newspaper articles and where to buy a feather like this."

"Why the different initials on the scorecard? "What has that got to do with Ryan and the feather?" Francy asked, shaking her head.

"Do you think this is happening because of the fundraiser tomorrow?" Della questioned.

"I don't know. But it can't be a coincidence that these showed up two days before the event. Someone doesn't want the fundraising to be a success." Lainey answered. "Francy, do you know what Shep and Vera are going to do for supper?"

"It's Friday and Shep is working at the Backwater until around 11p.m. Why?"

"I'd like to talk with both. How would the two of you like to meet at the Backwater tonight? I'm hungry for a piece of Shep's famous razzle berry pie!" Lainey grinned.

"Sure," Della answered. "What time?"

"I'll bring Mom along if she hasn't planned to be there anyway," Francy said. "By 9:30 p.m., most of the supper crowd is gone. Why don't we meet there then?"

"Sounds good. Let us help you put things away, Lainey." Della said.

"Thank you, but there isn't much to do. You two take off and I'll see you tonight."

It only took a few minutes for Lainey to clean the kitchen after her friends left. She was glad to have a few hours to gather her thoughts, make notes about what she already knew, and to find more information.

What's the connection here, Lainey? She sat down in front of her computer screen. *What are you missing?*

Chapter Three

The rest of the afternoon passed quickly, and Lainey hadn't found any additional information. Nothing stood out as a common thread. A prohibition raid on an underground bowling alley, an Indian feather with red paint spots, and four sets of initials had her stumped. She hoped Shep could shed some light on Gerry Hayward's past.

As she drove toward the Backwater, she noticed a definite chill in the air. The sun was setting earlier and earlier each day, bringing the reality that winter was approaching. Parking her car in front of the restaurant, she saw Charlie's Bait Shop off to the left. The lights were still on, and she wondered if he was making a fresh batch of stink bait to supply the fall anglers who fished late into the night.

She got out of her car, walked toward the Backwater, opened the door, and stepped inside. The smells of country fried steak mingled with freshly baked apples greeted her. The walls still looked new after the refurbishing paint work last year for the Governor's Fishing Opener. She looked around the cafe and found her friends sitting at a round table toward the back of the room. They waved as she walked toward them.

"Long time no see," Lainey kidded everyone, pulling out a chair next to Vera. "I hope I didn't keep you waiting. Okay if I sit here, Vera?"

"Of course, my dear. Shep can sit on the other side of me."

"He is bringing us a pie sampler plate," Francy said, rubbing her hands together. "I haven't had supper and I'm going to try a tiny piece of each one!"

"He spoils you girls, that's for sure." Vera rolled her eyes. "Good thing you know me!"

The ladies laughed loudly. They talked about the coldness in the air, about dreading the snow, and about the bowling tournament the next evening. Shep appeared with a large platter with samples of six dessert pies and a carton of vanilla ice cream. The ladies clapped as he put the platter in the middle of the table.

"Since this appears to be a special Whoopee meeting night, I thought you might need a little nourishment.

The pieces are blueberry pecan, chocolate coconut cream, cinnamon apple strudel with cream cheese, razzle berry delight, strawberry rhubarb, and Vera's favorite, sweet potato nutmeg. Enjoy!" One side of his mouth turned up in a crooked smile and he walked over to sit beside Vera.

"These look delicious! How about we cut each piece into fourths?" Della suggested as she picked up a knife and began cutting smaller slices of each pie. "Pass your plates!"

Shep watched and smiled as the Whoopee group took a few minutes to devour the pies and ice cream. He excused himself from the table, walked into the kitchen, and came back out with cups and a pot full of coffee.

"No dessert is complete until you have a cup of java." He handed cups to each of the ladies and poured piping hot coffee in each one.

"Hmm," Lainey said, smelling the coffee. "It's southern pecan, right?"

"You guessed it. My customers seem to prefer it." He sat down, looked at his watch and then at the ladies. "Vera tells me you want to talk about Gerry's bowling history. Is that right?"

Della and Francy each pointed one of their fingers toward Lainey at the same time. "We'll let her tell you." Francy said.

"Okay. I heard Bailee Ballulah came to see you this morning."

Lainey nodded and began telling Shep that Bailee had received a second envelope with an Indian feather and another scorecard inside.

"Say that again?" He leaned forward. His elbows were on the table and his hands were clasped tightly together. "The same frame was highlighted, but different initials were written inside it?"

"That's right. The initials were BB and GH. You have any idea why someone would target Bailee?"

Shep sat with a puzzled expression on his face. He unclasped his hands and lifted his palms in the air. "Wow, I'm at a loss. I can't think of any reason Bailee would be involved in anything."

"I asked her to search for stores that sold feathers like this one." She took a sip of coffee before continuing. "And I asked her to gather any additional newspaper articles regarding the charges against her father."

"Doc was bowling with Shep when the news broke," Vera commented. "He told me Gerry was extremely lucky to escape serving time in prison."

"I agree," Shep nodded. "It wasn't the first time Gerry had been involved in a scandal, either."

Francy, Della, and Lainey's eyes opened wide. They looked at each other, and then at Shep.

"You mean Gerry was charged with a gambling

offense prior to the PBA case?" Della questioned.

"No, no. It had nothing to do with gambling. Gerry had graduated and was sweet on a girl who was still in high school. Unfortunately, another local guy was interested in the same young lady."

"What happened?" Francy urged. "Was the girl Pheebs?"

Vera shook her head no. "I forgot about that incident, Shep. Poor young man. My father-in-law was the one who tried to save...what was his name again?"

"I don't remember right offhand."

"Are you saying Gerry fought with a guy over some girl? And the fight ended up killing someone?" Lainey asked.

"Not exactly. It was such a long time ago. I don't remember all the details. Gerry had taken a job as a maintenance guy at a small bowling alley by Redwood Falls to pay for college. He was working on one of the pin setting machines when the guy came into the alley to confront him. The other guy got caught in the machinery during their fight and bled to death."

"Oh my gosh. That's awful! The guy's family didn't press charges?" Della blinked in disbelief.

"I believe the coroner ruled it as accidental," Vera replied.

"Back then, there was no internet, or mobile phones or Facebook. Since no charges were filed, the town's people went about their day-to-day lives, not giving much thought to the incident. Gerry left the bowling alley and shortly afterward met Pheebs."

Silence fell on the group as no one really knew what to say. Francy finished her coffee and put her empty cup on the table. She looked at her mom and Shep.

"It's getting late, and tomorrow is the big event. You two," she pointed her finger at the couple, "You haven't told us about your costumes."

Vera crossed her arms in defiance. "And I'm not about to." She leaned her head toward Shep. "And he isn't going to either!"

"I can promise you that my little sweetheart has gone all out to win the costume contest," Shep assured the ladies. "She'll be the cutest…"

"Don't you dare tell them!" Vera interrupted him in mid-sentence. Shep rolled his eyes and nodded in compliance.

"It is getting late," Lainey chuckled. "Thank you, Shep, for the pies and for the information. I think I'm going to head home."

"Here, here!" Della said. "Best dessert in the country. I'm heading out, too."

"I brought Mom, so I'll stay till she's ready. You two be safe driving home."

"You're most welcome," Shep acknowledged. "Let me walk you to your cars."

Della and Lainey stood up and waved goodbye to Francy and Vera. Following Shep to the main entrance and into the parking lot, they waved to him, got in their cars, and drove away.

Lainey had gone straight to bed, still tired from the night before. The next morning, she slept in later than normal. Powie, impatiently letting her know he was hungry, had been walking and purring loudly back and forth on the top of her pillow. When she didn't respond, he laid on her head, ever-so-gently putting his paw on her face.

"I get it, Powie. I'm up, I'm up." She sat up, stretched, and yawned before looking at the clock on her phone. "Holy cow," she said to the cat. "It's almost noon! You need food and I need coffee!" She stood up, picked up her phone and headed toward the kitchen.

Powie trotted along beside her, still purring loudly, then sat by his food dish, waiting for her to fill his bowl. She made a cup of coffee, stood at the counter, and glanced at the to-do list she had put on her phone. Before the clock showed 1 p.m., she had finished her second cup of coffee, showered, dressed, and checked her work email. Thankfully, the inbox had nothing urgent needing her attention.

Lainey grabbed her fanny pack, walked into the garage, and slid behind the wheel of her KIA. She needed to visit two different grocery stores to cash in on the deals, as well as mail work items and buy cat food from the local pet store. She wanted to be back home by 5 p.m. That would give her plenty of time to get ready for the Holy Rollers fundraiser.

Lainey drove to the post office only to realize she had forgotten to bring the items she needed to mail. So, she drove back to her house to grab the items. Even with the second-round trip to mail things, she finished her errands and drove into her garage at 4:45 p.m. She carried the groceries inside, put them on the counter, and was busy putting them away when her cell phone rang. It was Bailee Ballulah.

"Hi, Lainey. Do you have a minute to talk?"

"Of course, Bailee. I always have time for you. What's up?"

"I had a hard time finding any place that sells that certain type of feather," she began. "I ended up asking Ryan."

"Oh. I know you didn't want to worry him about this. What did he say?"

Bailee paused. "He didn't show any feelings. Not anger. Not surprise. Nothing. All he said was if I wanted information, I needed to speak with his father, Binesi. Then he went to work."

"How do you feel about asking his father? I know you said you didn't have a great relationship with his family."

There was a longer pause and Lainey wondered if she had gone too far with her question.

"I apologize, Bailee. You don't need to answer that. I didn't mean to upset you."

Waiting a few more seconds before talking, the young bride cleared her throat. Lainey knew she was trying not to cry.

"No. It's okay. I want to share something with you that is bothering me."

"I'm listening. What is it?"

"At our wedding rehearsal dinner, I overheard a small portion of a conversation between Ryan and his dad. They mentioned something about blood revenge. I didn't think anything of it at the time." Her voice cracked and Lainey could hear her sniffle.

"Bailee, you don't need to…"

"I want to tell you." She sniffed a few more times before continuing. "Last week, his father came to visit him. They were in the front room, and I was making supper in the kitchen," she paused, then continued, "when I heard those words, blood revenge, again. This time I wrote it down to look it up."

"I'm not familiar with it. What did you find out about it?" She was making notes, too, and wanted to research more about this blood revenge.

"Hang on a second."

Lainey heard papers rustling while she waited for Bailee to speak. She didn't wait long.

"I found this on the internet, so I don't know how reliable or accurate it is. Blood revenge is the practice of seeking blood retribution. It's a theory where families, clans, or tribes are considered sacred communities. I guess when one member's blood was shed, it was like the entire community's blood was shed. Someone from that community would need to atone for the act by shedding the blood of the murderer. Do you think I should be worried?"

Lainey's stomach turned sour. Why would Ryan and Binesi be speaking about revenge? Something was wrong.

"Tell you what. It's 6:30 and we both have a Midnight Bowling event to get ready for. I'll keep working on this and you concentrate on enjoying this fun evening. How does that sound?"

Bailee sighed. "Okay. I need to get to Spare Lanes early anyway."

"What team are you bowling on?"

"I'm not bowling. Pastor Keegler asked me to help him with the registration table and prizes. We're giving away five large pizzas tonight in addition to the costume contest prizes. He wants to make sure everyone fills out a ticket."

The two finished their conversation and ended the call. Lainey had been looking forward to bowling again and hadn't realized how much she missed it. She walked into her bedroom closet to get her costume ready.

She had ordered a Star Trek Pin Badge, a pair of

Spock ears, and a red Star Fleet Cadet shirt. To complete her transformation, she cut the legs of an old pair of black yoga pants to mid-calf length and pulled up the only black socks she had, compression stockings. She laced her black tennis shoes and did a look-over. This would have to work!

Lainey pulled into the Spare Lanes parking lot at 10:15 p.m. The lot was already full, and she ended up parking on the street in front of the alley. She chuckled to herself when she got out of her car. Walking across the street ahead of her were a werewolf, Minnie Mouse, Iron Man, and SpongeBob SquarePants. A line that stretched from the front entrance to the sidewalk at the end of the street was filled with characters waiting to go inside. She took her place at the end of the line, behind a young girl dressed as Wonder Woman.

"I'm so glad to see this huge turnout," Lainey remarked to the girl.

"I heard that there were more signups than any other fundraiser Pastor Keegler has sponsored. Bailee and I were in the same graduation class in high school. Nice Spock suit!"

"Thank you!"

The line moved quickly, and within a few minutes, Lainey was able to stand inside. The entryway and walking areas were packed, and the air buzzed loudly with laughter and the sounds of people visiting. She could see Bailee, dressed as Pocahontas, sitting at the registration table, talking and greeting each person signing in.

When it was her turn, Bailee looked up from the table and blew out a big breath.

"It's been crazy, Lainey! Look at all these people. Pastor Keegler said he had people donate to stand like a gallery on television, watching and cheering on the bowlers!"

"I'm so glad. And your costume is terrific."

"Thanks. Now, please sign in and fill out your ticket for the pizza drawings. You're on lane 7. The rest of the Whoopee Pin Slayers are already here."

Lainey signed her name and slowly made her way through the crowd to lane 7. Sure enough, in full black dress suits with white shirts, black ties, black hats, and sunglasses, stood the Blues Brothers. They were laughing and talking when they saw her walk up.

"Spock, good to see you, man. Glad you made it!" Jake, aka Della, shouted.

"About time. We're gonna burn up the alleys tonight! Nice suit, brother!" Elwood, aka Francy, commented, trying to look cool.

"Your suits are…fascinating," Lainey replied with a monotone voice as she raised one eyebrow. She lifted her right hand, fingers pressed together, making a letter V, and said, "Bowl long and prosper!"

The three friends laughed and hugged each other. Lainey looked around, not seeing Vera or Shep.

"Where's your mom and Shep? I thought they'd be here early."

"Oh, they're here," Francy winked at Della. "Mom has Shep in the kitchen helping her with a last-minute wardrobe malfunction of some kind."

"We still haven't seen their costumes," Della said. "It's one of the few times Vera's kept a secret this long."

Lainey chuckled. "I need to get my bowling bag from Shep's locker. Save my seat. I'll be right back."

She made her way through the crowd toward the narrow hallway that had metal lockers on either side. Shep's locker was 231. She noticed the combination lock on the handle was not locked and thought he had left it open for her. She opened the door, took out her bag and shut the door, pushing the lock shut.

Making her way back to lane 7, she saw Pastor Keegler standing behind the registration table, still trying to get the last bowlers signed in. She sat down, unzipped her bag, and took out her purple Hammer. Smiling, she got up and put it in the rack around the ball return. She sat back down, ready to get the rented bowling shoes she had left in her bag since Thursday's practice, when the crowd noise elevated to a roar. She put the bag down and looked around. People on the lanes and in the entryway were standing, cheering, and clapping. Lainey stood and began cheering when she looked toward the kitchen.

There, in all her splendor, walked the Flying Nun, aka Vera, in her long, flowing black habit. On her head sat an oversized white cornette, the straight wings sticking out at least a foot on each side and turned down at the edges. They flapped up and down with each step she took. She was waving as if she was royalty. And walking beside her…was Lucifer, aka Shep, wearing a flaming red jumpsuit. Complete with two sparkly big horns on his head and a small red tail, he was carrying a pitchfork in one hand and a battery-operated fan, pointed directly at the Nun's flapping cornette wings, in the other.

"Holy smokes!" Francy giggled and clapped. "She is so in her element!"

Lainey laughed, sat down, and while the crowd was cheering, picked up her bag to retrieve the shoes. She froze when she looked inside the bag. There was a red envelope stuck inside one shoe.

Chapter Four

The Flying Nun and Lucifer completed their grand entrance walk and the crowd noise died down to a buzz once again. Shep, before going to his team on lane 5, put down the fan and held Vera's hand as she took her place on lane 7. He noticed the worried look on Lainey's face and questioned her.

"What is it? What's going on?"

"This was in my bowling shoe," she answered, pulling the red envelope out of the bag, and holding up it for him to see. "Did you leave your locker open for me earlier this evening?"

Shep shook his head no. "Spare Lanes had a few lockers vandalized this summer, and since then, I always use the combination lock. It was open when you got your bag?"

"Yes. I didn't think anything of it until now. How did someone get your combination?"

"Gerry keeps a list of everyone's combinations in his office. People forget those all the time. Someone must have had access to that list."

"Open it." Della urged. "We all know this is not a coincidence."

Nothing was written on the front or back of the envelope. Lainey carefully tore open one end and pulled out the contents.

"It's a girl's photo with an 'X' marked across her face," she said, handing it to Shep. She paused before opening the folded white paper, knowing what it was.

"That's another scorecard, isn't?" Francy asked. "Is it frame 4? Are there initials on it?"

"Yes, but only one set this time. The letters CD are in the pin count box, but the spare count box has a big 'X'."

Vera, looking over Shep's shoulder, gasped when she saw the girl's photo.

"You know her, Mom?" Francy asked.

"I think we both know who she is," Shep replied. "You remember, don't you, Vera?"

"My goodness. When I saw her face, everything came back to me," she nodded slowly.

The noise was growing louder, and the bowlers were anxious to start. Lainey moved closer to Shep and Vera before talking.

"Who is it? What did you remember?"

"It's Lois Hermann. Her mother, Mabel, and I were good friends," Vera commented sadly. "Such a pretty young thing."

"Her dad, Vernon, bowled with us," Shep added with a grim look on his face. "After she died, he was never the same."

"How did she…" before Lainey could finish her question, a loud squeal came across the speakers, causing everyone to wince. The tournament was beginning.

Shep put the two items back into the envelope and handed them to Lainey. "Put this in your bag for now. We'll talk later tonight."

"My apologies! We're trying to correct the feedback issue. Give us one moment!" Pastor Keegler, acting as emcee, said over the squealing. He was dressed as Marc Antony in a white, bedsheet toga cinched at the waist with a gold tapestry cord and tassel. On his head was a wreath of greenery that was spray painted gold.

Shep made his way over to lane 5 where his team, The Pocket Pounders, were waiting for him. The Whoopee Pin Slayers were quietly putting on their shoes, all wanting to know the details about Lois. There was a tapping sound on the mic.

"Testing, testing," Pastor Keegler said. "I think we have it fixed!" There was a spattering of applause and a couple of whistles in approval. He cleared his throat and raising his left hand in the air, began his welcome speech.

"Friends, Romans, and Bowlers, lend me your ears! Welcome to the Holy Rollers Tournament at Spare Lanes Alley!" He waited for the clapping to stop before continuing.

"As you know, this is a Midnight bowling fundraiser for our dear friends and owners of the alley, the Haywards. Let's get them up here for a minute. Gerry and Pheebs, where are you?"

There was applause, but neither Gerry nor Pheebs appeared.

"I'm sure they are busy in the back making sure you have a fun time bowling tonight," Keegler stated, giving them a few more seconds to appear.

"Tonight, we are not only giving a prize for the best costumes, but to celebrate the world-famous pizzas made right here in the kitchen, we're giving away five large ones tonight!"

The audience clapped and he motioned for Bailee Hayward to come to the mic.

"Pocahontas did a great job getting everyone registered, don't you think? Let's give her a big hand."

Bailee, carrying the box with the pizza tickets inside and looking a bit uncomfortable with the attention, smiled, and waved.

"Since the pizzas take a little time to cook, we decided to award them now, so you have time to order.

Here are the lucky team winners!" He reached into the box, pulling out the 5 tickets.

"When I call your team's name, send one person up to get the coupon from Bailee. The winners are the Bowling Stones, the Curve Bowlers, the Lane Busters, the Deadwood Blasters, and last but not least... Strikes R Us!" People laughed and cheered as each team sent a member to retrieve the free coupon.

"We will announce the costume winners at the end of the evening. Let's go over a few rules. Each team will have fifteen minutes to throw practice balls. Bowlers must bowl in the order listed on the score screen. When the practice time is over, the lights will go out leaving only the black lights on each lane. And yes, before Frank on the Retired Rollers team asks, we will keep the lights on for you to find the restrooms!"

Laughter broke out and a man at lane 18 raised his hand and saluted. Pastor Keegler laughed and bowed.

"There is one more item that we need to address before we begin," he said somberly. "Each bowler please stand up. Look at the person on your right. Good. Now, look at the person on your left." He paused slightly. "Pick the one with the best smelling breath, give them a hug, and wish them good luck!"

The bowling alley filled with laughter and chatter.

"Bowlers, we are starting the lanes. Your fifteen minutes of warmup begins now."

The sounds of balls hitting pins and resetting

machines filled the air. Lainey threw a practice ball, still not able to concentrate fully on bowling. She was waiting for her ball to return when she heard loud screams coming from one end of the alley. Turning her head, she noticed everyone had stopped in their tracks. Several had their hands over their mouths in shock. It was as if they were frozen in time.

She saw Shep and Charlie Crowfoot, who were assigned to lane 5, running down lane 4 toward the pins. Pastor Keegler was running down the side of the building to the machine room. The pin setter had lowered and instead of grabbing pins, it was stuck in the down position…with a human arm hanging from the top of it.

Chad Devon, who was bowling on a different lane, walked to the mic at the registration table. His voice sounded calm.

"Please, everyone, stay where you are. I've called 911. Wait at your lane until further notice."

Shep and Charlie knelt on the lane, looking up into the setter machine. Lainey's first instinct was to get to that pin machine. People's attention was focused on lane 4 and no one seemed to notice as she walked calmly down the small path next to the outside wall that led to the machines. She walked through the curtain door and could see Keegler standing behind a machine, his hands on his hips. He looked up to see her walking toward him.

"Wait!" He raised his hand to stop her. 'You don't want to see this."

She didn't stop. She wanted…no, had to see. When she reached lane 4's machinery, it was no longer spinning like a clothes dryer drum. It had stopped because the body of Gerry Hayward was wedged into its gears.

EMT's arrived within minutes and police Captain, Ben Sargent, followed. The bowling alley was strangely quiet. Over the next hour, instead of costumed characters laughing, bowling, and having fun, medical and police personnel hurried in and out. Lainey had gone back to lane 7 to let her friends know what had happened.

She talked softly, explaining what she had seen. Vera's face turned white when Lainey mentioned Gerry. Francy took her arm and helped her sit down.

"It'll be alright, Mom," she tried to reassure her.

Vera sat with a blank look in her eyes, shaking her head slowly in disbelief.

"Della, have you seen Bailee? Or Pheebs?" Lainey asked. "I want to get to them before they hear from someone else."

"I haven't even thought to look." She stood up and looked toward the registration table. "I don't see either of them. Chad is standing in the front talking to one of the police officers. He might know."

Lainey began walking toward Chad and the officer

and noticed that Ben Sargent was walking toward them from the opposite end of the building. He reached the two first.

"Chad, I need to use the mic. We've got to get these people out of here in an orderly manner," Sarge stated.

"Yes, sir." He picked up the mic up, turned it on, and handed it to the captain.

Once again, a brief, loud screech over the speakers got everyone's attention.

"Folks, we are requesting that you please gather your personal items and leave through the west entrance door. Do not wander through the building. Officer Denton will release you by lane numbers. Go directly to your cars and head to your homes. We will be contacting you for statements, if needed. Thank you."

The captain handed the mic to his officer. He turned, and motioning for Lainey to follow him, walked toward the lockers.

"Shep mentioned that the Haywards had received threats of some kind the past two days. Did you not think to tell me about them?"

"Gerry got the first envelope Thursday night, and he dismissed it. When I found the third envelope tonight, my intention was to bring them all to you in the morning. Honest."

The captain glanced around and frowned. "I had Officer Roark take Bailee and Pheebs home for now. I want those envelopes to me tonight. Do you have them here?"

Lainey shook her head no. "The first two are at my house. I've got the third one in my bowling bag."

"Good. I'm going to be busy here for a while. I'll text you when I'm at the office. Bring them to the station. It's going to be a late night for all of us."

"Okay. How did Pheebs take the news?"

"Surprised and shocked. Bailee fell apart. Officer Roark called her husband to let him know what happened and to pick her up at her mom's house." The captain's pager went off and he nodded to Lainey before walking toward lane 4. "Watch for my text."

Lainey stood for a couple of seconds, not wanting to be seen leaving at the same time. Her friends were waiting for her at lane 7. Shep had joined them.

"Sarge said you told him about the envelopes," she looked directly at Shep. "He wants me to bring them to the station tonight. You were back there while the EMT's worked on Gerry. What did Sarge or the EMT's say?"

"Once they realized he was dead, the conversation turned to speculation on how he became entangled in the first place. The machines are older, and it would only take a second if someone weren't paying attention to get an arm stuck in the revolving barrel."

Francy shivered. "It's hard to imagine having your arm severed. Poor Gerry."

Vera, who had been uncharacteristically quiet, took a deep breath and, looking toward Shep, shrugged her shoulders. "There is much to discuss, but I think we should leave now. We can meet at my house. I'll make a pot of coffee."

The group gathered their things and agreed to meet at Vera's. An officer was still directing people out the designated door and into the parking lot. Each walked to their cars in silence and within twenty minutes, were parked in front of their friend's house. Inside, Vera made a pot of coffee while the ladies gathered around her kitchen table.

"Where is Shep?" Della asked. "I saw him come inside."

"I asked him to get something for me. It's in the attic in the garage," Vera answered. She looked at Francy who was staring at her.

"You sent him to the attic? The only things stored there are Dad's," she commented, her eyes narrowing. "What's he looking for?"

Her mom didn't respond.

Lainey, having taken the red envelope out of her bowling bag before getting out of her car, opened it and placed the photo and the scorecard on the table.

"Vera, do you have a notepad and a pen? I want us to review what we know before I see Sarge." Lainey stated.

"I always keep at least one note pad and pen in my

kitchen junk drawer. When I think of something I need from the store, I write it down to keep from forgetting. I'm not a spring chicken anymore, you know!"

The ladies smiled at her attempt to lighten the mood. She opened the drawer, took out a pad and pen, and handed them to Lainey.

"Thank you," she said. She drew three columns on the page and labeled them Envelope one, Envelope two, and Envelope three.

"What do we know about the first envelope? I want to write everything down," she said to the ladies.

"I thought it was odd that Gerry blew it off," Francy said. "Wouldn't you question a strange envelope that was given to you?"

"Agreed. We know the photo was in the basement of The Church of the Ascension and where bootleggers went to smoke and drink," Della added.

The coffee was ready, and Vera brought cups to the table. She poured each a cup while they were talking. Francy noticed that her mom kept looking toward the garage door, waiting for Shep to come inside.

"And we know the letters PH are for Phineas Hayward, Gerry's grandfather. He was a reporter that spied on bootleggers, giving their location to the police." Della finished.

Lainey nodded, writing down bullet points. "The newspaper article was about a raid the police did at that location. And one person was killed during the raid. But we don't know who, correct?"

Della shook her head no. "I'll do more research on that tomorrow. There must be death records somewhere."

They heard the back door close and watched as Shep walked toward the table, setting a dusty records box in front of Vera.

"If this isn't the right box, I'll look again. I blew off as much dust as I could and according to the label, it would be about the right year."

Vera nodded and stood up. She leaned over the top of the box to read the faded black plastic label.

"I remember using a dial labeling machine every year to close out Doc's files." She rubbed her finger over the white raised letters. "Let me see if it's in here."

She untied the tattered brown twine around the box and took the lid off. Everyone around the table was standing, straining to see. Crammed inside were yellowed file folders with a tab on each one. The ink on each was faded and Vera began thumbing through them.

"Mom…what are you looking for?" Francy asked impatiently.

"I'll know when I see it. Give me a few minutes."

The ladies looked at each other, then at Shep. He motioned for them to sit down and clasped his hands together on the table to wait. Francy sighed and, resting her elbows on the table, put her chin in her hands.

"Envelope two..." Lainey suggested, changing the conversation back to the list. She wrote down the words Bailee, feather, and blood revenge.

"All I know is that it contained a feather and a scorecard had initials of BB and GH," Della commented after taking a big sip of coffee. "Bailee was going to research where to buy the feathers, right?"

Lainey realized she hadn't told her friends about the phone call from the young bride earlier that morning, the troubling relationship with Ryan's father, or anything else. She pursed her lips and wondered how much she should share at this moment. Before she could decide, Vera took out a file from the box and waved it in the air.

"Whoop! I knew it would be there!" She looked at Francy who still had her chin in her hand. "Kids…" she said to Shep, "they always want things in a hurry!"

The ladies laughed and Francy raised her chin and grinned.

"Exactly what is that file?" she asked.

"Your dad kept very good records of his patients. Details from birth to death. If he treated someone, he kept a record of it. He was old school and felt a responsibility to each person or family." She opened the file and pulled out several handwritten pages. She smiled and her eyes teared up. Blinking quickly, she hoped no one noticed. "He was a good man…and the best doctor in the world."

"My husband said he was genuinely loved by the community," Della remarked. "I know you are proud of him."

"Yes, very proud," Vera replied. "The reason I asked Shep to get this file is because of the photo in the red envelope." She paused, waiting for one of them to speak.

"With all the chaos surrounding what happened after we opened the envelope, I forgot that you recognized her. What did you say her name was?" Lainey had her pen ready to write it down under the column for envelope three.

"Lois Hermann. This is Doc's file on Lois. Birth to death."

Chapter Five

Vera handed each of the ladies a few pages from the file. It would be faster if they each read them while she and Shep shared what they knew.

"Little Lois Hermann was not the most popular girl in high school. She was what kids today call a book nerd," Shep began, "on the honor roll, in the school band, and she sang in the church choir. Your all-round-girl-next-door."

Vera nodded. "She was a year behind Gerry, and I remember how upset Mabel was when he began to show interest in her. He was arrogant and would get angry quickly. Some thought he was a bully."

"That's interesting." Francy poured herself another coffee. "Gerry wasn't exactly who Mable wanted her daughter dating."

"No, he wasn't. Mabel felt she knew what was best for Lois and forbade her to see him. But he was very persuasive, and she started to lie to her parents about staying late at the school for practice or study for some test."

"That's a very common story," Della smiled. "Kids have been doing that forever."

Lainey had been listening and trying to decipher the handwriting on the few pages Vera had given her. There was an entry that she thought read 'treated for a broken wrist.'

"Can you read this entry? Does it say Doc treated Lois for a broken wrist?" She handed the page to Vera who held it close to her eyes.

"Yes, it does. Doc didn't have the greatest penmanship. He wrote the injury was from a fall during band practice." She handed the page back to Lainey. "See that little asterisk out to the side? That means that Doc had doubts about her explanation of the accident."

"Hmm...this happened about the same time she was sneaking out to meet Gerry."

"Per the date of the entry, which would be about right."

"Oh my gosh. I bet she's the girl Gerry fought over!" Della blurted out.

"That's what we think, but her name was never mentioned, and Gerry never admitted to dating her."

Shep rubbed his hand across his forehead. "This is a small town. Most people knew it was Lois."

Lainey put down her pages and looked at the others. "If Lois was the girl, who was the other boy? And what happened to her after Gerry killed him?"

"I wonder if this broken wrist entry was about the same time as the fight where the other boy was killed. While I'm searching death records for the bootlegger, I'll see what I can find on this mystery guy," Della stated. "I'll get on that first thing in the morning."

"Thanks. That would help a great deal. But we still need to figure out envelope two and why the feather," Lainey commented. "Any ideas?"

"My first thought was that the initials BB and GH were for Bailee Ballulah and her dad. But the feather puzzles me," Francy admitted.

"I thought that, too," Lainey agreed. "I haven't had the chance to tell you that Bailee called me this morning. She decided to tell Ryan about the envelope."

"I bet he was upset. If my new husband got a threatening envelope or letter, I'd be upset for sure," Della remarked.

"Oddly, Bailee said he showed no emotion at all. He told her to speak with his father if she wanted to know more," Lainey replied hesitantly. "Ryan's family hasn't embraced her either. In fact, it sounds like his father resents her for some reason. He ignores her."

"That is disheartening to hear. She is so sweet and

now that her dad has been murdered, she's going to need Ryan to lean on," Vera said in a sad tone. "Can you talk with him, Shep?"

"I will speak with him, but ladies…" he paused as he thought carefully about his next words. "Their marriage is none of our business. We can be there to help support Bailee, but…" he heard Vera's voice and instantly regretted his choice to speak.

"But? But what?" she interrupted, her voice growing louder with each word. "Are you saying we're a bunch of busy bodies?" She crossed her arms and stared at him.

"Sweetie, I meant I'll talk to him, that's all." He stood up and gave her a big hug. It was easy to see that her anger softened at his touch. "It's been a very long day and we're all tired."

"You're right," she smiled up at him. "Sometimes I can get a little defensive."

"And a bit bossy," Francy laughed. "We still love you, Mom."

"Shep is right." Lainey looked at her watch. "It's 2 a.m. I doubt that Sarge is going to call me this late anyway."

"I agree. I'm exhausted. Let's get some sleep and plan on meeting tomorrow. Want to meet at Babe's for coffee around noon?" Della asked.

Lainey shook her head no. "How about meeting at my house? It's more private than talking at Babe's. I'm sure the entire town will be buzzing about this. Hopefully by noon I will have talked with Sarge, and we'll have a little more information."

"That works. You two head home. I'll help Mom clean up," Francy said.

"Thank you," Lainey replied as she gathered her notes and walked toward the front door. She turned to say goodnight and remembered the box of files.

"Oh, Vera! Can I bring the file for Lois with me? I'd like to read all of it again."

"Of course, dear." She put the papers back in the file and handed it to Lainey. "If you can't read Doc's writing, just make a note and I'll decipher for you later."

Lainey was confused and exhausted. She'd intended to stay up to look through the file Vera had given her, but knew she needed sleep to clear her mind and start fresh in the morning. She got ready for bed and plugged her cell phone into its charger. Before she could turn off the bedroom light, her phone rang. It was Sarge. He sounded tired, too.

"I know it's late," the captain began, "but I need you to be in my office at 8 a.m. Bring the envelopes and all the information you or the Whoopee group may have found. I know your friends are helping on this."

"I don't have that much yet, but I will bring my notes…and the envelopes." She paused, almost afraid to ask the next question. "Do you have any preliminary information about Gerry?"

"Now Lainey," his voice scolding her like a child, "it will take some time to get the coroner's report. You know that." His voice relaxed a little. "We can talk about it in the morning. We both need sleep."

"I'll see you in a few hours. Get rest, Sarge."

The call ended and Lainey set her phone alarm for 6 a.m. The last thing she needed was to oversleep. She turned off the light and laid her head on her pillow. In what seemed like a matter of minutes, she heard the alarm sounding loudly. She had slept soundly for a few hours, at least.

She quickly showered, dressed, and sat down with her cup of coffee to look through Doc's file before meeting at the station. Vera was right about one thing. Her late husband had terrible handwriting! The file wasn't large, but the faded ink and yellowed pages made several entries unreadable. She flipped page by page, thinking there wasn't going to be much to go on.

It was then that Lainey saw a photo, one that might have been taken with a Polaroid instant camera. The snapshot was stapled to the page and had faded badly. Her skin began tingling and the hair on her arms stood up. She knew Sarge would want to know about the folder and that he would keep it. Wanting more time to research, she took out the page and put it on her office desk.

Lainey put the envelopes, the folder, and her iPad into her backpack. She left her house and walked into the police station shortly before 8 a.m. The dispatcher buzzed her in, telling her the captain was expecting her. She walked quickly to his office and was surprised to see his door closed. She knocked, wondering who was inside. Sarge opened the door and motioned for her to sit in the chair to the right of his desk. She couldn't sit in the chair left of his desk because Pastor Leon Keegler occupied it.

"Lainey, you know Pastor Keegler," Sarge said walking behind his desk and sitting down. "He is here giving me updates on Phoebe and Bailee."

"Yes, hello Pastor," she greeted, holding out her hand to him.

"Hello. Terrible about what happened last night," he answered, shaking her hand weakly. "I'm sorry you had to see poor Gerry's body."

Lainey cut her eyes toward Sarge, who was frowning. "I thought maybe I could help Shep and Charlie."

"If there is nothing else you need, Pastor, I have much to do." Sarge stood, his eyes still on Lainey.

"Of course," Keegler replied. "I'll be in touch if the family needs anything. Thank you for seeing me this morning." He shook hands with the captain, nodded to Lainey, and left the room.

"Want me to close the door, Sarge?" Lainey offered, trying to avoid his anger.

"Yes," he replied, his eyes still intently watching her.

She walked over to close the door and then returned to her seat. It was awkward having him glare at her in silence. She opened her backpack and took out the envelopes and her iPad. She left the folder inside for the moment.

"I did go back to the machine room when I saw Shep and Charlie. I needed…"

Sarge held up his hand to stop her. "You didn't touch anything, any machines, or the body, did you?"

"You know I wouldn't do that," she tried to sound insulted. "And no, I didn't take anything from the room, either."

His frown slowly disappeared, and he sat forward in his chair. "Let's start with the envelopes. Gerry received the first one on Thursday at your bowling practice, correct?"

Lainey nodded and handed Sarge the first envelope. She gave him a moment to examine the scorecard and the newspaper article. When he looked up, she explained what Della had found about the basement church bowling alley being the bootleggers meeting place. She told him that Phineas Hayward, Gerry's grandfather, was a spy for the police department, and about the raid that was documented in the newspaper article.

"Are you thinking the PH on the scorecard is Phineas Hayward?" Sarge asked.

"It seems very possible. A person was killed during that raid and Della is researching records to find out who," she said, then instantly regretted her statement.

"Della is researching what database?"

"Online public records. She has an extensive background in genealogy and may have other databases."

"Are you planning on raiding my files again, using Vera's treats to disguise your sneaking into my office?"

Lainey shook her head no, but she smiled despite trying not to. "We haven't done that since the investigation of the murders of Raymond Sullivan's brothers."

The captain put the scorecard and photo back in the envelope. "Where's the next envelope?"

She handed it to him and again waited for him to examine what was inside. He ran his fingers over the feather, then put it down and looked at the scorecard.

"The pattern on the scorecard is the fourth frame, am I correct?" he asked her. "I assume the last envelope also has something highlighted in that frame?"

"Yes, it does. And Gerry's body was found in the machinery on lane 4," she mentioned. "I think it is more than a coincidence, don't you?"

Sarge nodded. "It might be. Now, where did you get this envelope?"

Lainey took a deep breath. She told him how it had been taped to Bailee Ballulah's car and the feather was like those in her husband, Ryan's, headdress.

"I asked Bailee to find stores where feathers could be purchased…" she wrinkled her nose and pursed her lips before continuing. "And I asked her to get more information on the PBA charges against her dad."

Sarge put down the feather and raised his eyebrows. "You've obviously failed to mention information to me. What makes you think Gerry's issues with the PBA are relevant here?"

Lainey shared that Shep had been involved in the bowling community during that time. He knew that Gerry was charged with gambling and trying to persuade bowlers to lose on purpose. Instead of going to prison, the PBA had compassion for his family and banned him for life.

"Bailee didn't go into the details but mentioned how embarrassed she had become and that Pheebs had grown to hate Gerry."

"Why do you stay that?"

"She overheard her parents arguing recently, and Pheebs said that to him," she finished speaking, running her hand up and down the strap of her backpack, fidgeting. Sarge noticed.

"There is more to this second envelope, isn't there," he said calmly. "I'm waiting."

"Shep said that Gerry had been involved in an

incident while he was working his way through college," she began. "He had been dating a younger high school girl that another young man was also fond of. The two men fought, and the other man died…" Lainey's face flushed, and her eyes opened wide. "Holy cow, Sarge! It just dawned on me! Gerry was fighting with this other young man at a bowling alley – in the machine room. Somehow the young man got caught in the machinery and bled to death before anyone could help him!"

Sarge blinked a few times, then opened his desk drawer and took out a notepad. He wrote down a few things while Lainey watched him. He picked up the scorecard again, studied it, and then wrote more notes.

"Does Shep know the name of this young man? Was Phoebe the girl they were fighting over?" he questioned.

"He couldn't remember, but Della…" again the captain interrupted her.

"We will investigate this, Lainey. What about the girl? Was it Pheebs?"

"No, it was not," she picked up the third envelope and handed it to the captain. "This is the envelope, the red one, that was left in my bowling bag before the fundraiser. It has a scorecard and a photo."

He picked up the envelope, emptied the two items and studied them. "The 'X' on the girl's photo is alarming." He looked at the grin on Lainey's face. "You know who she is."

"Vera and Shep both recognized her. She's Lois Hermann."

Sarge made more notes, then looked at the scorecard. "Only one set of initials on this one. And it's the only envelope that is red, correct? You haven't received anything else since last night?"

She shook her head no. Her gut said to bring out the folder Vera had given her, but she was hesitant. After seeing the captain intently studying the photo, his organized mind trying to find a common thread, she decided to give it to him. She opened her backpack, pulled out the old folder and slowly laid it on his desk.

"What is this?" He looked at her, then at the folder, then back to her. "I thought you said you had not received any more envelopes or information."

"Vera recognized the photo you're holding as Lois Hermann. She remembered that Doc had treated her and her family. This is Doc's old file on Lois…from birth to death."

"Death? Lois Hermann is deceased?"

"Honestly, I have not had a chance to look more deeply into this file, but according to Vera, yes, she passed away a long time ago. Vera was friends with her mother. It's odd that she has an 'X' across her face."

"And the initials, CD…mean anything to you or Vera or Shep?"

"I know these are clues, but there has to be more than we are seeing," she sat back in her chair. "Where do we go from here?"

"Everything you brought is evidence in an ongoing murder investigation case," he said as he gathered the items. "I've known you a long time and I'm sure Francy and Della are searching for names or other items. I'm requesting that if you find anything, you tell me about it immediately. My team will begin following all these leads as well."

She nodded. "I do know Della is trying to find the name of who was killed in that bowling alley raid and who the young man was that fought with Gerry. I promise, if she finds these before you do, we will tell you."

He took a deep breath and blew it out…twice. "Lainey, trouble seems to find you, whether you are looking for it or not. I must warn you again. Murder is complicated. Whoever killed Gerry had a detailed plan that could have taken months or years to develop and carry out. Make no mistake, this was deliberate. If a person or persons commit one murder, they will not hesitate to commit more to keep from being caught."

She nodded. "I agree with you that Gerry's murder was not a spur of the moment action. I've been thinking of how Bailee and the feather fit into the murderer's plan. What's your first impression?"

"My first impression is to not make assumptions

until I have further evidence," he said, watching as she rolled her eyes at his response. He gave a slight smile and added, "My gut tells me you have more information about the feather or Bailee." He crossed his arms, not moving his gaze away from her eyes. "What is it?"

Lainey bit her bottom lip. She was struggling with herself, deciding whether to ask him about blood revenge or not. Rubbing her forehead with her left hand a couple of times, she swallowed hard.

"Sarge, how well do you know Binesi Ballulah?"

He uncrossed his arms and sat forward in his chair. "The Ballulahs are good people and long-time residents in the area. I've met Binesi several times in passing and around town, but I don't know him beyond that. Why?"

"Bailee told me that he hasn't welcomed her into their family. In fact, he doesn't speak to her," she paused to gather her thoughts. "She overheard him talking to Ryan a couple of times mentioning the words 'blood revenge.' Ever heard of that?"

"It was a process that was used to resolve animosities between Native American groups or clans that resulted when one individual killed another." The captain's forehead wrinkled, moving his eyebrows closer together. He didn't try to hide the look of concern that covered his face. "But I've only read about it in history books."

"Me, too. Why would Binesi hold a grudge against

Bailee? Could it be that she wasn't the one he wanted Ryan to marry?"

"Right now, we can't speculate on anything, and even though she mentioned it to you, it's hearsay, not hard evidence." He stood up and walked toward the office door. "Now, we both have things to do. Thank you for coming in. You *will* stay in contact with me, understand?"

Lainey stood up, and as she walked out the office door, nodded. "Yes, sir. I will."

Chapter Six

The cuckoo clock on Lainey's kitchen wall was striking 11 a.m. as she walked inside from the garage. The Sound of Music was her late husband's favorite movie and he had given her the clock on their last anniversary. She smiled as she watched the clock door open and a little bird poked its head out, chirping eleven times. When it retreated into the clock, the chorus of Edelweiss began playing while a door opened underneath the bird's perch. Seven little Von Trapp children twirled and swirled to the music on a carousel. Out one door and in the other, every hour on the hour. Powie was meowing and rubbing against her leg trying to get her attention. She picked him up and he turned on his purring motor.

"I can't hold you all day," Lainey grinned, stroking the top of his head. "The Whoopees will be here shortly, and I have to fix something for them to eat," she said putting him down. He whined letting her know he was feeling rejected, turned his backside to her, and sauntered over to perch on the cat tree. "Don't give me attitude, Powie. You get enough attention!"

She walked over to the pantry, opened the door, and stared at a jar of crunchy peanut butter, a few cans of baked beans and chicken. She said aloud, "Looks like the ladies will have to make do with grilled cheese sandwiches today."

The doorbell rang before she could start fixing lunch. She opened it to see Francy and Vera standing on the porch with a large bucket of Kentucky Fried Chicken and a six-pack of Diet Mountain Dew.

"We thought we'd bring lunch today," Francy said as she walked inside. "Mom was hungry for coleslaw."

"Why thank you! I was going to make grilled cheese for us, but crispy fried chicken sounds yummy," Lainey replied. "What's with the Diet Mountain Dew cans? You two starting to drink that now instead of coffee?"

"I won these, fair and square," Vera stated proudly. "It's the anniversary of the restaurant opening some twenty years ago and if you bought a bucket of chicken today, you could spin a prize wheel they had."

Francy shook her head slightly and smiled. "Mom is the luckiest person alive. There were only three prize spaces on the wheel with nine others saying 'Sorry, try again.' Her spin landed on the Mountain Dew prize."

"Well, congratulations, Vera! Thank you for sharing your prize with us."

"No need to thank me." She set the six-pack down on the counter. "I'm not going to drink this diet stuff. All those bubbles make me sneeze. Besides, coffee keeps me young, you know."

"Has Della called you?" Francy asked. "She was going to be here early."

"She hasn't, but I'm sure…" the front door opened, and Della rushed in before Lainey could finish her sentence. She was trying not to drop her computer, several over-filled folders, her purse, a water bottle, and her cell phone.

"Stop the presses!" Della hurried through the kitchen. "You're not going to believe what I found this morning!" She dumped everything onto the counter, spilling papers from the files and almost knocking over the large bucket of chicken. "Lunch can wait, girls. I know names!"

The ladies grabbed chairs from the table and gathered around the counter. Della was busily flipping through the papers that had fallen from the files, mumbling to herself.

"If you're going to mumble, turn up the volume," Vera said a bit perturbed. "I can't hear a thing you are saying!"

"Here they are. I made a copy for each of you," Della almost shouted. "Remember the article and photo of the church basement where Phineas Hayward was a spy for the police?" She pushed the copies toward her friends. "And we wondered who was killed during that raid?"

Lainey nodded yes, studying the copied page she had been given. She skimmed down the page and saw an obituary. She raised her eyebrows and looked at Della. "Claude Cooper?" she asked. "CC as in frame 4 of the scorecard?"

Della crossed her arms in triumph. She had a smile on her face as big as a Cheshire cat cartoon. "Absolutely! Claude Cooper owned a small grocery store near Olivia. And he was known as a major bootlegger in Renville County."

"That's great. But how does that connect to Gerry Hayward? Other than his grandfather was behind the raid," Francy wondered. "Does the obituary give any clues?"

Della fumbled through a couple other pages in the folder before speaking. Lainey noticed that Vera's eyebrows had grown close together and the corners of her mouth turned slightly downward, betraying a troubled look on her face as she read the obituary. Francy noticed it too.

"Mom?" Francy questioned carefully. "I've seen that look on your face many times. You know something you're not telling us."

Vera laid the paper down. Putting her right elbow

on the counter, she covered her mouth with her hand. She was deep in thought when Della spoke.

"I checked through public marriage records and found that Claude Cooper was married to Zella Brown. Her family were farmers and owned, at that time," she paused to read notes she had written on the page she was holding, "they reportedly owned more than two hundred acres."

Lainey said as she sat back in her chair. "How does that tie in?"

"Zella was their only child. Shortly after her wedding to Claude, her father died of a heart attack. Her mother died a year later. Zella inherited all that land."

"So good old Claude became rich," Francy commented. "Are you thinking that is how he funded the bootlegging business?"

"I have no idea, but, according to county records, the Brown farmland was sold to the county soon after the mother's death. Part of it was developed into what we know today as Hwy 212."

"What did the county do with the rest of the land?" Francy asked.

"Apparently, they sold it off over the years and or rented to other farmers," Della continued.

Vera sat very still, listening and was unusually quiet. It was obvious that she was deciding whether to speak. Finally, she wrinkled her nose and spoke.

"Zella Cooper went to the same church as my parents," she began. "She never recovered from Claude's death. Once it was known that her beloved spouse was nothing more than a hoodlum selling liquor illegally, she was shunned by many in the area. Poor Zella became more and more of a recluse over time. She died only a few years after Claude."

The ladies were quiet for a moment, each trying to figure out how the information tied in with Gerry or his family. Della opened her computer, turned it on, and waited for it to quickly boot up. It chimed, signaling it was ready to serve her commands, so she began typing.

"What happened to the money Zella had when she died? Had Claude spent the money the county had paid for her family's farm? We're missing something here…" Lainey muttered. "Why did the scorecard have Claude's initials on it and why was it given to Gerry?"

Vera cleared her throat. "Zella didn't have children, but her aunt had a son. She left some of the money to the church, and the rest to the aunt's child."

"In the obituary, it lists under survivors an aunt from her mother's side of the family. The image is so blurry, I can only make out the first name of Faye," Della commented. "I'll keep searching."

"No need," Vera said quietly. "Faye Keegler was the aunt. Her son's name was Ralph. He was the beneficiary of what Zella had left."

The three ladies sat in silence, confused, each trying to absorb what they had heard. Della typed in the search bar the name of Ralph Keegler, hoping to find out more information. As the minutes passed, each of the friends knew what question needed to be asked.

"Is Ralph related to Pastor Leon Keegler?" Lainey broke the silence. "Vera, do you know?"

"Yes, Ralph was Leon's father. Before you jump to conclusions, poor Zella had very little to leave him. If I remember correctly, he inherited her little house and a little bit of savings."

"I pulled up Ralph's obituary," Della commented. "It's odd that it was only a few lines long and didn't say much about his life."

"Well," Vera replied in a matter-of-fact tone, "suicide isn't something newspapers like to print."

"Oh my gosh," Francy commented. "That must have been hard on Leon. How old was he when his father died?"

"I'd say in his late teens. Ralph thought he was a shrewd businessperson. He tried, I don't know how many times, to get Doc to invest in some scheme he was working on. Your dad was bright and knew any investment Ralph was involved in was doomed. If he did have money at one time, he blew it away on foolishness."

"Do you know if that is what caused him to kill

himself?" Lainey asked. "Perhaps he was in debt over his head or something like that?"

"I'm not sure about that. Back in the 50's, few people invested in the stock market. It was still recovering from the big crash of 1929. There were very few stocks to invest in and those were expensive. There was no internet or way to get information quickly. Stockbrokers were very rare and charged outrageous fees. Many were flat out dishonest."

"And you think Ralph fell into the investment trap and couldn't get himself out?" Francy asked.

"Yes, I do, but I don't know that for a fact. I remember seeing him a few days before he died. He came by Doc's office to ask for a loan. He looked sad, unkept, and much older than his actual age."

"Wait a second…his obituary doesn't list his wife's name as a survivor," Della remarked. "Did she divorce him or something?"

"She had an affair and divorced him when Leon was still a youngster. I have no idea what happened to her," Vera stated.

"From all indications, Pastor Leon did not have a great childhood," Lainey began. "And I'm sorry for that. However, the chances of tying family relationships between Claude Cooper, Phineas Hayward, Zella Brown, and Ralph Keegler to Gerry's murder are slim. Much of this information could be considered consequential. It's not hard proof."

"I say we take a break and eat," Vera said with sudden renewed energy. "That tub of coleslaw is calling my name!"

The ladies agreed and spent the next half hour devouring lunch. Della was the only one who decided to try Vera's Diet Mountain Dew prize. She popped open the pull tab and poured the yellow-green liquid into a glass filled with ice.

"Hmm..." she commented. "No fiz. That tells me this Dew is flat." She tasted it and grimaced. "Yep, flatter than a pancake." She looked at the can for an expiration date and found none.

"For pity's sake," Vera said angrily. "How dare they give me a defective prize! I'll take this back and they can give me a fresh six-pack."

"Mom, it's just soda," Francy laughed. "You don't even like Mountain Dew."

"It reminds me of Seven-Up," Vera grumbled. "My mother made us drink it anytime we were sick. Didn't matter if I had a sore throat, skinned my knee, broke a bone, or was dying from the plague. Seven-Up was her cure all. Yucky!"

Lainey giggled. "How about a cup of coffee? I have French Vanilla, Cinnamon Spice, and Breakfast Blend flavors."

"Breakfast Blend will work. Can you pour this out?" She handed her glass and empty pop can to Lainey. "I'm sticking with java from now on!"

It didn't take the group long to clean up after lunch. Lainey had made a fresh cup of coffee for each of them while Della logged back into her computer.

"I haven't had much luck finding the name of the young man that fought with Gerry at the bowling alley," Della said with disappointment. "You'd think there would be a record or death notice or something."

"I'll see if Bailee can let me into their archives. There may be some small article or write up about it, too," Lainey said. "We know it was within a couple of years after Gerry graduated from high school and before he married Pheebs."

"I suppose that narrows it down a bit," Della answered. "As much information as these public sites have on births, deaths, marriages, and divorces, it's hard to imagine the records we are looking for have disappeared."

"Thinking about Bailee," Francy raised her first finger on her left hand in the air, "have you decided to speak with Ryan or his father? I know you asked Shep to talk with him."

"I'm debating on that. I don't want to make things worse for Bailee," Lainey answered, "but I feel the person I need to speak with is Ryan's dad, Binesi. Vera, do you know if Shep has spoken with Ryan yet?"

Vera shook her head. "I don't know. They had a large wedding reception last night and I haven't seen him yet today. I plan to meet him for supper, though. Why don't you stop by and ask him yourself."

Lainey laughed. "You think Shep will listen to me like he does you?"

Vera grinned and blushed. "Well…he'd better if he knows what's good for him!"

The ladies shared a good laugh and finished their coffees. Francy looked at her watch and stood up.

"Guys, I told Marcie I'd fill in at dispatch for her this evening. It's her anniversary and Denny is taking her out to a fancy restaurant and winery."

Lainey immediately thought about Sarge's comment earlier that morning. *'Are you planning on raiding my files again, using Vera's treats to disguise sneaking into my office?'* With Francy working at the dispatch desk, tonight would be a good night to snoop around.

"Are you filling in on the afternoon shift or night shift?" she asked her friend.

"It's the 3 to 11 p.m.," Francy replied, then added slyly, "Are you going to visit me?"

Vera's eyes opened wide. "I still have my black cat burglar suit and I can take some strawberry rhubarb bars out of the freezer!"

"It's amazing," Francy said, rolling her eyes. "Mom is hard of hearing, unless you are talking about Shep or breaking and entering!"

Lainey grinned. "No, we're not needing to play cat

burglar in Sarge's office…" she winked at Francy. "Not tonight anyway. But thank you for offering."

"Okay. Then I will plan to see you at the Backwater, yes?" her eyes squinted as she stared at Lainey. "I'm taking out the bars just in case you change your mind!"

Lainey's plan for the rest of the afternoon was to complete paperwork on a couple of cases she had been assigned for work. Her investigations were over and now her task was to write, edit, rewrite, and re-edit her final reports. She had learned years ago that while drafting a final report was not always her favorite part of the job, the documentation was extremely important and could make or break a court's decision in a case. An hour had passed when she was interrupted by her cell phone. The caller's ID told her it was Bailee Ballulah.

"Hello, Bailee. Your ears must have been burning because I planned to give you a call later this afternoon. What's going on with you?"

"Today is Ryan's birthday. I had planned a little party for him and invited a couple of friends to come this evening. The plan was to cook burgers and hotdogs on the grill, with cake and ice cream for dessert."

"What a nice thing to do. I'm sure he will enjoy that."

"He informed me an hour ago that his parents are also coming…and bringing a few of their relatives who attended our wedding. Not ten minutes after that, both couples I invited called and cancelled."

"What reason did they give you for cancelling?" Lainey's instinct told her Ryan was behind the cancellations.

"One couple said their child was sick. The other said they had been given courtside tickets for the Timberwolves basketball game tonight. I'm worried about being alone with his family. They will ignore me. Will you come? I mean, at least I would have someone to talk with."

Lainey heard the pleading and desperation in Bailee's voice. She, too, was worried. But not about Ryan or his family or the so-called friends who cancelled. She was worried about Bailee.

"I'd love to come," Lainey said calmly, trying not to show how concerned she was. "What will you tell Ryan about my coming?"

"You wanted to look up things in my work's archives, remember? If you *happen* to stop by while his parents are visiting, he can't be upset with me. I have access to all those files on my home computer."

"What time should I *happen* to come by?"

"They will be here around five. Could you come between five-thirty and six?"

"I will be there! And Bailee, I'd like to meet his parents. Would you feel comfortable introducing me to them?" Her mind was racing. This would be a perfect way to observe Binesi and Ryan and their interaction with Bailee.

"I can," she hesitated, "but they may not acknowledge or greet you."

"That won't bother me," she reassured. "I've dealt with mean or rude people before."

"Thank you so much," her voice cracked. "You don't know how hard I try to…" her voice faded out and Lainey could hear her crying.

"Don't you worry! I'll be at your home no later than six. We'll visit, do a little bit of research on the computer and I'm more than happy to help you eat the cake and ice cream!"

Bailee laughed. "Thank you. I'll see you soon."

The call ended, but the slightly nauseous feeling in her stomach that developed when Bailee called didn't. In fact, it was growing stronger. Would she be able to get Binesi to speak with her or even greet her? She hoped so.

Ryan and Binesi…you won't know it, but I will be all ears, especially if you mention the words blood revenge.

Chapter Seven

The afternoon sky had turned from partly sunny to cloudy and stormy. Strong thunder boomers, as Lainey's mother used to call early fall rain and windstorms, were rare around Mirror Falls. But on those occasions when they did occur, thunder roared continuously while lightning bolts bounced like laser beams back and forth between dark grey clouds. When a lightning bolt strayed from its routine pattern and struck the ground, the powerful charge from the bolt lit up the area and, for a second, it was as if it were daylight again. Then, as predictable as the day always turns into night, a loud booming noise that shook the rafters of houses followed.

Lainey was never fond of dreary, rainy days or the lack of sunshine that accompanied them. Those bleak few weeks in February, when the sun never came out of its hiding place, made even the smallest problem appear to be the size of Mount Everest. She needed to see the sunshine, to feel the warmth of it. Many people were happier when the days were brighter, and she felt the same way.

As she drove toward the Ballulah's home, the heavy rain had turned into a light, drizzly mist. Lainey had spent time reviewing her notes about the envelope Bailee had received a few days ago. The one thing that she hadn't paid much attention to at first were the few red spots on the feather that was in the second envelope. She hadn't received the third envelope at that time, but today, the word *red* stuck in her mind. Was it just a coincidence that the last envelope was red and the dots on the feathers were red? Or was she reading way too much into it? As Sarge mentioned to her that morning, the killer had been very deliberate in planning Gerry's murder. She felt strongly that the color had to be a clue.

Lainey's plan for her visit with Bailee was to meet her in-laws and get a feel for Binesi and his personality. She knew he wouldn't be too welcoming, but she hoped to stay within earshot when doing 'research' with Bailee.

There were several cars parked in the driveway of the couple's house. Lainey decided to park on the street, ensuring that she could leave quickly if she needed to. She walked up to the house, rang the doorbell, and was shocked by the person who answered. It was Charlie Crowfoot.

"Hello, Lainey," the familiar voice said warily. "We weren't expecting you. What can I do for you?"

"Hello, Charlie. I stopped by to see Bailee. Is she here?" She gathered her composure quickly, hoping Charlie hadn't seen her surprised look.

"She is, but I'm not sure this is a good time. It's Ryan's birthday and we're having a family party."

"Oh, I see. I didn't mean to crash your gathering," she fibbed. "Can I speak with Bailee for a moment? It won't take long."

Charlie paused, studying her face intently. She held his gaze, knowing he was looking for any signs of mischief or untruth. Finally, he blinked, and took a couple of steps backward into the front room.

"Sure. Come inside. I'll find her." He didn't motion for her to sit down but turned and walked through the small entry hall into another room. He had left the front door open, which she knew meant her stay would be short. She stood inside the front door entry, looking and listening.

The little house appeared to have been built in the late 1970's and even though it had been updated, the blown-in popcorn ceilings were not vaulted, and no longer white, but a dingy grey. It made the room seem smaller than it was. Lainey smiled when she looked at the paneled walls. Each 4-foot-wide piece was supposed to look like knotty pine. Her parents' house had the same exact paneling.

"Hello, Lainey!" Bailee walked toward her. She cut her eyes to her left quickly. Charlie was standing directly behind her. "What a surprise to see you! Come inside and sit for a while."

"Thank you. I apologize for barging in on you. I didn't realize you were having a family get together. If this is an inconvenient time, I'm happy to come back." She gave the girl a hug as Charlie watched closely.

"You're welcome anytime," Bailee answered, still playing her part well. "What is it you need?"

"Could you help me access the newspaper's archive files. You mentioned you could do that from your computer?"

"It's Ryan's birthday and his family is here to help celebrate. But I'm sure I can take a couple of minutes to help you. Don't you think, Uncle Charlie?"

It was obvious that Charlie was taken by surprise by Bailee's question. He shrugged slightly, and his answer sounded forced.

"That's up to you," he muttered. "Maybe you should check with Ryan."

"No, that's not necessary," Bailee said with a forced

giggle. "Lainey, you're welcome to use my computer. I'll help you." She turned slightly so Charlie could hear her next words clearly. "Let me introduce you to Ryan's family. They are in the dining room, and we were getting ready to have cake and ice cream!"

"Thanks, Bailee. I promise not to take much of your time."

Lainey watched Charlie closely. He was smart and she didn't think he believed her visit was simply a coincidence. She needed to be careful around him. While she never had an altercation with him directly, he knew she was good friends with Shep and Vera. Add the Governor's Fishing Tournament incident a few years back, and she could see why he would question her presence tonight.

Always keep your enemies close by...even if you aren't sure they are enemies.

She followed Bailee down the short hallway and into the dining room. The conversation that had been going on stopped abruptly when she entered the room. Sitting around a square picnic-type table were Ryan and his parents. The table had benches on the sides instead of chairs. On each end was a larger chair that looked like it was made from tree branches. The seats were covered with a beautiful handmade quilt or blanket. Binesi sat in one, and Ryan sat in the other.

The three stared blankly at Lainey and then turned their gaze to Bailee. She smiled and nodded.

"Everyone, this is Lainey Maynard. She is a friend of mine who stopped by to use my computer and I invited her to share cake and ice cream with us."

Dead silence. No one said a word or changed their expressions.

"Lainey, please let me introduce Ryan's father and mother," Bailee added. "This is Binesi and Shaniah Ballulah."

"Hello everyone. It's nice to meet you," she walked over to Binesi and put her hand out to shake his. He did not respond. She took a few steps toward Shaniah and offered her hand. The woman nodded slightly but did not offer to shake hands.

She walked to the other end of the table to greet Ryan. He stood up and shook her hand.

"Father, Lainey is friends with Shep Morton. And Uncle Charlie knows her as well."

Binesi looked intently at her, then seemed to relax a little bit. He nodded to her but did not smile.

"Thank you for inviting me to share cake and ice cream with you to celebrate your son's birthday," she said. "May I sit by you, Mrs. Ballulah?"

The woman's back straightened and Charlie quickly stepped in.

"Lainey, you can sit by me."

"Thank you, Charlie." She had hoped the tension in the room would diminish, but it didn't.

"Great!" Bailee said as she walked into the kitchen.

"I'll dish up the cake and ice cream while you visit. It will only take a moment."

If Lainey were sitting naked in a room full of popes, nuns, and pastors, she would have felt less awkward than she did at the table. No one spoke. No one looked around. So, she decided to push her luck.

"Ryan, Shep tells me you are quite the chef! Do you enjoy working at the Backwater?" She asked.

"It's a new challenge, but I've always enjoyed cooking," he answered after looking at his father to get permission to speak. "Shep is gracious to teach me what he knows."

"I love his razzle berry pie," Lainey smiled. "He has been in business a long time. Do you want to own your own restaurant some day?"

Again, he looked briefly at his father before answering. "I'm not sure what my plans are, but I'm happy to be training with him."

Lainey could see this conversation was leading nowhere. She decided to take a chance and direct a question to Ryan that was aimed at getting Binesi to speak.

"Do you have other aunts and uncles beside Charlie? Or other brothers and sisters?" From the corner of her eye, she saw Binesi's mouth draw up into a straight line. He moved in his chair, and Ryan didn't speak. She waited for an answer, hoping the silence would make one of them uncomfortable enough to speak.

Bailee came back into the room carrying a tray with the cake and ice cream. She had heard Lainey and made a point to answer.

"Ryan doesn't have any siblings," she said pleasantly, setting the tray in the middle of the table. "I think he's perfect so there was no need to have any more children." She grinned, walked over to her spouse, and bent down to kiss his check. He impulsively pulled away.

Bailee, embarrassed, looked toward Lainey and backed away from Ryan. "Let's see how good this Dutch chocolate cake is with our favorite vanilla bean ice cream." She served each one a bowl with cake and ice cream. No one spoke. The only sound was the clinking of spoons hitting the sides of the bowls.

"That was great cake, Bailee. Thank you! Chocolate is one of my favorites," Lainey smiled. She understood why Bailee felt so uncomfortable around Ryan's family and she was disappointed in Charlie, too. Why wouldn't he at least thank her for the dessert?

"You're welcome," she replied. "Let me clear the dishes and we will get on my computer." She got up to clear the table.

"I'll help you," Lainey said. "Charlie, are you through with your bowl?"

He nodded yes and handed her the bowl. Bailee picked up the other bowls and the tray and the two walked into the kitchen. Putting her finger to her mouth, she motioned for Lainey not to speak as she put the tray on the counter. There was no door between the kitchen and the dining room. Anything the two said would be heard by all.

"Thank you, Lainey. I'll wash these up later. Let's go to the spare bedroom. That's where my computer is."

"Great," she replied, playing along. They had to go back through the dining room into the hallway to get to the spare bedroom. Once inside the room, Bailee closed the door and spoke quietly.

"These walls are so thin. We will need to speak softly in case one of them tries to listen in."

Lainey gave her a hug. "Dear Bailee, I'm sorry they treat you so badly."

"It's okay. I started thinking it was my imagination," she whispered. "Now, what are you needing to look up?"

Bailee sat down in front of her computer to log in. Lainey, looking around the room for an extra chair, noticed a few photos on the wall. She walked over to look at them.

"Bailee, who are the people in these photos? Are they Ryan's ancestors?"

"Yes," she answered, getting up from the computer.

"These are the only photos I found of his family. I'm surprised he hasn't made me take them down."

"Is this Binesi when he was young?" she asked, pointing to a photo of two young boys standing in front of an old fence.

"Yes, Binesi is on the left and that is his brother, Baako, standing next to him."

"I thought Binesi had no brothers. Remind me again where Charlie fits in?"

Lainey listened as Bailee told her that Baako was Binesi's younger brother. He was killed in some sort of accident when he was a teenager and Ryan's family rarely spoke of him. Binesi's dad had a sister who was Charlie Crowfoot's mother.

"Charlie really isn't Ryan's uncle, but my understanding is that after Baako died, Binesi and he became as close as brothers," she said. "You know it's odd. Even with my dad's gambling addiction, my parents were always kind to others. How could they run a bowling alley if they never spoke to people?" She turned and walked back to her computer. "I'm resigning myself to the fact that Ryan's family may never accept me."

"How did you find out about Baako? I mean, did Ryan tell you about him?"

"No. Charlie told me one day," she said sadly. "He found me crying, holding those few pictures I had found in a box Ryan had in his closet. He felt sorry for me."

The two didn't speak for a moment. Lainey pulled up a chair and was sitting next to Bailee when her computer finished booting up.

"Now," Bailee said while typing. "I need to know what kind of records you are looking for. Birth, marriage, death? It makes a difference which archive I enter."

Lainey's original plan was to look through death records in the hope of finding who Gerry Hayward had fought with so long ago. She doubted that Bailee knew about that fight, and she certainly didn't want to be the one to tell her. After seeing how the Ballulah's acted toward her, the last thing she wanted was to cause the young bride any more pain. Her father had just died, and she was living in what looked like a bad marriage. She had enough on her plate to deal with.

"I don't want to keep you very long and perhaps cause trouble between you and your in-laws. Can we look through birth and marriage records for a person named Lois Hermann?"

"It's really no problem. If I were in the dining room, they would ignore me anyway," she answered as she typed in the name. Within a few seconds, Google had produced several entries on Lois Hermann. The first one was a death record.

"Here is an obituary for Lois Hermann. If this is

correct, she was only twenty-three when she died. Want me to print this page out?"

"Yes, please! I was told she had passed away, but I didn't know at what age. Was she married?"

"The obituary only lists her parents and a son."

Lainey's mouth fell open. "She had a son? Does it give his name?"

"No. But we can look at birth records and see what we can find."

Bailee's fingers typed away quickly, minimizing screens, and flipping back and forth between directories. Within minutes, she clicked open a birth record.

"It's a hospital record so it only shows a baby boy born to a Lois Hermann. I'll print that for you, too. Poor dear. If she was twenty-three when she died, according to this hospital record, she was only seventeen or so when the baby was born."

"Was the hospital in Mirror Falls?" Lainey asked. Back in the day, if an unmarried girl gave birth, she was sometimes sent away from her hometown to avoid embarrassment for the family.

"No. It was a small-town hospital in South Dakota. Let me search for it. The name of the town was Baxter."

"You're very quick on the computer," Lainey remarked. "I'm glad you are doing this for me."

"No problem," she smiled. "The hospital and the

town closed years ago. Today, there is no place called Baxter in the state. Is there anything else to look up?"

Lainey smiled. "You have helped more than you know. Thank you, thank you!" She walked over to the printer and took the pages Bailee had printed. "I really should be going."

Sadness fell over the young woman's face and Lainey's heart broke for her. "Bailee, I have an extra bedroom, you are more than welcome to come and stay with me."

"You are very kind," she said, blinking to hold back tears that were forming in her eyes. "Ryan isn't as bad when his parents aren't here. I'll be fine. I've met with Pastor Keegler a couple of times, too. He is very understanding."

"How is your mother holding up? This must be a difficult time for both of you."

Bailee shrugged her shoulders. "Mom is fine. I've not even seen her cry about Dad. I worry that she is in shock or something."

Lainey nodded, but her thoughts were not about Pheebs being in shock, rather about feeling relieved that Gerry wasn't in her life anymore.

"I'll try to check on her tomorrow. Now, I've got to be going."

Bailee opened the bedroom door, and they were not surprised to see Ryan turn quickly and walk toward the dining room.

"See," she whispered to Lainey, "it's not the first time I've caught him listening to my conversations!"

"Remember," she cautioned Bailee, "I'm serious. If you need a safe place to stay, call me. Promise?"

"Yes. He's harmless, really. I'm sure his dad puts pressure on him or something."

As Lainey walked past the dining room toward the front door, she paused long enough to wave and say once again that she enjoyed meeting everyone. No one answered, but Charlie got up from the table and walked toward her.

"Let me walk you to your car, Lainey," he said.

"Thank you, Charlie. I'd appreciate that."

The two walked out the front door and were to the curb where she had parked when Charlie spoke.

"I have nothing against you, Lainey," he began. "And I have nothing against young Bailee either. But Binesi is old school and lives by his family's traditions. Nothing will change that. It's best for all if you don't come back to the house to visit. They are a young married couple, and you know it takes time to get to know each other's quirks and habits. Give them some space."

For a moment, Lainey thought she saw worry on Charlie's face. As ornery as he was with Shep and Vera, he seemed genuinely concerned.

"I don't understand it, but I will respect your wishes for Bailee's sake," she stated. As she opened her car door, she had a thought. She could ask him about blood revenge. "Charlie, I'd like to speak with you tomorrow. Can I come by your shop?"

Surprised, he nodded. "Sure. Is Shep sending you to spy on my new stink bait recipe?" He smiled and she laughed.

"Not this time, but if he and Vera decide to moon you again, it won't be my idea!"

Chapter Eight

Lainey got in her car and drove to the Backwater Restaurant. She hoped the dinner rush would be over, allowing Shep time to visit with her. She was able to park close to the entrance, and as she got out of her car, she noticed that a light was shining from Charlie's bait shop's back door.

I know Charlie is still at Bailee's house. Why would he leave the lights on in the backroom? Glancing at her watch, and knowing Vera wouldn't be expecting her yet, she walked across the parking lot toward the bait shop. The front entrance door was locked and the neon sign in the front window flashed 'Closed. Come back soon.'

Lainey walked carefully around the side of the building, toward the back door. There were no sounds or signs of life. She knew that the back door was meant for deliveries and for special anglers who drove their boats to the ramp behind his building. Tonight, no boats were docked there. She stood in front of the door, tried to open it, but it was locked. Standing on her tiptoes to look inside the window, she could see boxes on the floor, a couple pairs of rubber boots, a few white bait buckets, and an old desk with papers on it. Nothing that stood out to her as odd.

"You said you were *not* spying on my new stink bait recipe!" Charlie's voice boomed loudly causing Lainey to trip as she turned quickly from the door. He didn't offer to help her get up but stood with his hands on his hips looking down at her, frowning.

"Oh! You startled me!" she said, standing up and trying not to look guilty.

"I'm sure I did. Shep put you up to this, didn't he?" He said with disgust. "You tell him…"

"Wait…" she began after dusting the dirt off her pants and shirt. "Shep doesn't know I'm here. I went to the Backwater for supper and saw the light was on. I knew you weren't here and wanted to make sure no one had broken in." She hoped that didn't sound as lame to him as it did to her.

"You think I believe that?" He didn't move or change his expression. He reached inside his pants pocket, pulled out a set of keys and walked over to open the back door. "We're not going to wait till tomorrow to talk. Since you are so concerned about my shop, let's go inside and find out why you are here."

Charlie opened the door and motioned for Lainey to follow him inside. She wasn't afraid of him, but questions and answers were swirling around in her mind faster than a spinning centrifuge. This would be the only chance she would have to talk with him about Ryan and his father. Her first thought was to pull her phone from her fanny pack and hit the record button on their conversation. She was reaching for it when he stopped her.

"No one takes photos of my bait shop," he cautioned her. "Many have tried to see the ingredients for my bait, but none have gotten away with it."

Lainey smiled and, trying to ease the tension between them said, "Believe me. I am not at all interested in the ingredients."

He looked intently into her eyes. "You said you wanted to talk with me in the morning. You're here now, so talk."

"Do you have a place we can sit down?"

He nodded. "Come into my office," he said walking in front of her. "It's in the next room."

He flipped on a couple of lights and Lainey followed him into the small office. It was neat as a pin. Pictures of fishing buddies holding their catches, dates listed on each one, were placed on the walls in chronological order. There had to be a hundred or more. She couldn't help but marvel at them.

"Wow, Charlie! These pictures are amazing. You've been at this a very long time!"

"More than forty years. Many of these friends have moved away or passed away," he said quietly, sitting down behind his desk. "These memories are my whole life."

She couldn't help but feel a bit sorry for him. As much as he and Shep had quarreled over the years, and as mean as people thought he was, tonight, she saw loneliness in his heart.

He cleared his throat and the harshness of his voice returned. "What is it that you want. It was no coincidence that you came to see Bailee this evening. You've got five minutes to explain."

Lainey sat down, thinking about what information he might know and what information she didn't want him to know. She took a deep breath and blew it out. Then an idea hit her.

"I didn't see a picture of Gerry on your wall. Was he an angler?"

Charlie was obviously startled by the question and that was the reaction she had wanted. Her goal was to get him to drop his guard.

"Gerry? I have no idea if he fished. If you have questions about the murder, talk to the police."

"I wondered how close you two were, especially

since his daughter married your nephew." She watched closely as he sat forward in his chair, his eyebrows wrinkled.

He knew she was playing a cat-and-mouse game of some kind, but about what, he wasn't sure. His right eye twitched as he studied her face. She sat patiently, smiling as if they were discussing something as trivial as the weather. Finally, he broke the silence.

"Bailee is a sweet girl. She loves Ryan. And whether Gerry and I were close has no bearing on that."

"Does Ryan love her?" Lainey knew that was a bold question and that Charlie could shut the conversation down and force her to leave. But she also knew she had to cut to the chase.

He grimaced and nodded his head slowly. "She's told you that Binesi isn't friendly to her. Well, you saw that firsthand tonight. What business is that of yours?"

"Were you aware that Bailee received an envelope shortly before her dad was murdered?"

Charlie didn't reply.

"Inside was a feather, just like the ones in Ryan's headdress. Do you know anything about that?"

"No, I don't," his voice was strained. "Why do you think I would know anything?"

"You are Ryan's uncle. I would think if you cared for either of them, you might be concerned about threats made against them."

"What threats? A feather isn't a threat," he stated flatly. "How did you come up with that conclusion?"

Lainey paused, not taking her eyes away from his face. She weighed her next words carefully.

"But blood revenge is," she said slowly, bracing herself for an angry response.

Charlie was stunned. His eyes opened wide, and he stood up quickly. Instead of speaking, he paced back and forth across the little space behind his desk. He stopped, started to speak, then began pacing again. Lainey sat patiently, watching him squirm. She'd wait for him to answer if it took all night.

Finally, he stopped pacing and sat down in his chair. He took has right hand and ran it through his hair, taking a deep breath at the same time. Then, leaning back and folding his arms, he spoke with a calm voice.

"You are intelligent and a researcher," he began. "I'm sure you've discovered the meaning of blood revenge. It was, as you know, a longstanding tradition that dates back generations. Why do you mention it?"

Lainey studied his face a long time before answering. He must have known that Ryan and his father had discussed it. And he must know why Binesi treats Bailee so badly.

"I'll ask you again," Charlie led, "why did you mention blood revenge?"

"Binesi and Ryan have talked about it several times," she answered. She sat forward in the chair, looking him squarely in the eyes. "Bailee overheard them. I believe you also know the envelope had a bowling scorecard inside with the initials BB and GH."

"Yes, Ryan told me."

"Let's cut to the chase here, Charlie," she said forcefully. "GH, Gerry Hayward, has been murdered. Blood revenge conversations have been going on between Ryan and his dad…and I think you were included, too."

"Watch it, Lainey. If you are accusing people of murder, you better be darn sure of your facts," he said coldly.

She sat back in her chair. "Tell me. You're not really Ryan's uncle…are you."

"I can't say it's been a pleasure, but our little talking time is over," he stood up slowly and walked past Lainey to his office door. "I believe you said you were eating supper next door. You'd better go before they close for the evening."

She stood up and walked past him toward the shop's back door. Before she left, she turned and said, "You were right about one thing. Bailee is a sweet girl who deserves happiness. She's not to blame here. I hope you remember that."

Lainey walked out the back door and over to the Backwater knowing she had ruffled Charlie's feathers. She would let him stew for a couple of days before talking with him again. And the next time, she would bring Sarge with her.

The Backwater had only a few patrons and she saw Vera sitting at a back table as she came inside. She hurried over to the table, anxious to speak to Shep about Ryan. But the conversation quickly turned in a different direction.

"I thought you were going to stand us up!" Vera said, pulling out a chair for Lainey. "Where have you been?"

"I saw Bailee briefly this evening and then stopped to talk with Charlie over at the bait shop." She smiled, knowing that would get a rise out of her friend.

"You were at the bait shop? What is that old buzzard up to now? Shep says he been concocting a new stink bait for ice fishing," she said nonchalantly. "As if we care. Locals know Shep's standard bait will keep those darn walleyes biting this winter."

"I was there talking about Bailee and that envelope she had received. Is Shep coming out of the kitchen soon?"

"He's finishing up. Want to go to the kitchen and talk with him?"

"Sure. I hope he has a couple of leftovers I can munch on!"

The two walked to the back of the restaurant and through the swinging kitchen door. Shep looked up from washing dishes and greeted them with a big smile.

"Finally, the Whoopee cavalry has arrived to help me clean up." He took his hands out of the dishwater and dried them. "Are you hungry, Lainey? I still have a little bit of chicken noodle soup left. Let me get you a bowl."

"Yum! I need a hot bowl of soup about now," Lainey answered. "I had a little run in with your neighbor."

"You went to see Charlie? At the bait shop? Why? That place is a real dive," he said pouring steaming hot soup into a large cup. He opened a drawer and pulled out a soup spoon. "Here you go. Sorry, but I'm out of crackers."

She smelled the soup and grinned. "You make the best food! Thank you so much."

"She wants to know if you spoke with Ryan. Isn't that right, Lainey?" Vera said impatiently.

"No, I haven't seen Ryan today. He took off because his family was having a birthday party for him."

Lainey was hurrying to finish the soup and before she could tell them about being at that party, Vera had walked over to Shep and whispered something into his ear. He nodded, then went into the back supply room.

"Where did he go?" she asked. "I wanted to tell you both that I…"

Shep reappeared carrying, of all things, a large envelope. Lainey groaned out loud.

"Oh no…don't tell me this is a fourth envelope?" she asked in disbelief.

Vera chuckled. "Of course not! We have some information about Lois that you will want to know."

Shep opened the envelope and laid the contents on the counter--newspaper clippings and a couple of pages from a high school yearbook. Lainey put down the soup bowl. She picked up the yearbook pages and looked at them carefully.

"These are the school picture pages and I see Lois on the first one. But I don't recognize anyone on the second page."

"Look at the bottom of that second page, underneath the student photos," Vera commented. "Take a good look." She smiled at Shep, and he winked at her.

There were two photos at the bottom of the page. One showed a group of students sitting in the cafeteria talking and eating lunch. The other was of two students standing behind a desk in the library, helping other students standing in front of the desk check out books.

"It looks like Lois was working as a library aide? I think that is her picture behind the desk, correct?"

Shep nodded. "Yes. Do you know who is standing with her?"

"I don't recognize him. But he is handing a book to another student."

"That young man standing next to her is…" she paused, teasing her. "Shep, you tell her!"

"It's none other than our very own Pastor Leon Keegler. And the boy he's handing the book to is Gerry Hayward."

Lainey's mouth opened and she held the page closer to her eyes. "Crime-a-nellie! You're right. That does look like Keegler!"

"We found these in the library archives. Did you know they have newspapers from the early 1900's?" Vera said as she handed a couple of pages to Lainey. "Back then, everything went into the newspaper."

"We saw an article about old Robert Hayes, my neighbor and local ice cream truck driver. He would list the varieties of ice cream he had each week. Boy, did he serve great strawberry ice cream pops," Shep licked his lips. "I'd forgotten about him."

Lainey held up a clipping showing three couples standing together. One couple wore crowns. "Homecoming king and queen?" She asked. "Gerry must have been popular to be voted king."

She looked through the other articles, and while they mentioned Gerry, she wasn't sure how much of this was tied to Lois or the murder.

"I appreciate you both getting this information, but other than the photo in the library, how does this tie in with Lois?"

"Look at the last article. Two students are dressed

as clowns for the fall carnival. Read the names in the caption," Vera told her. "Lois is there and she's standing next to a Ballulah."

She stared at the names and then at the two people in the photo. She looked up in disbelief.

"Baako Ballulah. Did you know that he was Binesi's brother?" she asked her friends.

"How did you know?" Shep questioned. "Ryan has never spoken about him."

Lainey explained that she had gone to visit Bailee and to get access to the newspaper files she had on her computer. She mentioned how rude Binesi was, and that Charlie had been at the birthday party, too.

"We were waiting for her computer to boot up. I saw a few of Ryan's family pictures. Bailee had found them and hung them on the wall," she looked down at the clown article once more before continuing. "There was a picture of two young boys. One was Binesi and the other was Baako. Bailee said he'd died in some accident when he was a teenager, and that the family never mentions him."

Vera and Shep looked at each other, then back at Lainey. No one spoke for a moment as each tried to wrap their minds around this latest information. Then, as if a light bulb went off above his head, Shep almost shouted out loud.

"Are you thinking what I'm thinking?" he asked the ladies.

"Do you really think Lois and Baako liked each other?" Vera shook her head. "The Ballulahs were nice people, but I don't think Lois's mother would have approved of him."

"Lois's mom didn't approve of Gerry, either, but she snuck out to see him," Shep replied. "What's your thought, Lainey?"

"I think Della needs to search for Baako's obituary. I'm willing to bet it was about the time good ol' Gerry was working at a bowling alley."

She felt that familiar tingling on her arms and her instincts told her Baako was the young man Gerry had killed. If that turned out to be true, why would Binesi wait all these years to murder Gerry for blood revenge? And why would he go to such lengths to create three threatening messages?

"By the way, did either of you know that Lois had a son?"

The surprise was evident on both faces. Vera was the first to speak.

"What? Doc didn't have a record…" she stopped in mid-sentence and looked at Shep. "Goodness! That would be why Lois left Mirror Falls and never came back. I can't believe her mother didn't tell me or Doc."

"She wasn't married, Vera, and if she was expecting at that time, she probably left out of embarrassment," Shep consoled her. "It's not that her parents were hiding something from you."

"Well, what's the boy's name? How old is he? Where is he now?" she asked Lainey, obviously frustrated by this news.

"I have no idea. Bailee looked up the obituary for Lois and it said she was survived by a son. She did find a birth record in a hospital in Baxter, South Dakota. It only said baby boy born to her."

"It's getting late and I, for one, need time to process all this," Shep stated. "Vera, aren't the Whoopees taking supper over to Pheebs tomorrow?"

"Oh, yes, we are. Lainey, I forgot to tell you. Can you bring a potato salad? We're going to meet at her home at 5 p.m."

"Sure. I will be there." She wanted to speak with Pheebs anyway.

"Say," Vera said as an afterthought, "you said you had a run in with Charlie tonight? What was that about?"

Not wanting to say much more about Charlie and the blood revenge issue, she quickly answered that he thought she was there to steal his new stink bait recipe.

"I saw the light on in the back room and thought someone might have broken in," she hoped her explanation would appease her friends. "And he thought I was trying to steal his recipe for Shep."

Vera immediately puffed her cheeks in defense. "How dare he think Shep or anyone else would want to steal that…that pile of oatmeal he calls stink bait!"

Shep laughed and gave her a big hug. "That's my girl! Always come out fighting mad to protect me."

Vera snuggled into his hug. "You know what they say. If you can live through stink bait wars, you can live through anything!"

Lainey left the Backwater and on the way home, she called Francy to set up an appointment with Sarge for the next morning.

"Been busy this evening, Francy? Or have things been quiet?"

"Nothing too exciting going on. Mirror Falls is quiet. Are you coming by?"

"I thought about it, but I really need to see Sarge first thing in the morning. Can you check his calendar and see if he has anything going about 8 a.m.?"

"Give me a second. Gonna put you on hold and look."

Lainey had pulled into her garage when Francy returned to the phone.

"According to his schedule, he will be here. He does have a city council meeting at 9 am. Want me to put your name down for eight?"

"Yes, I do. I'm thinking he needs to go with me to visit Ryan Ballulah's father."

"You need to fill me in! But I've got to go right now. Seems no one has a problem until I am on the phone… then the whole switchboard lights up! Talk with you later."

The call ended and Lainey walked into her house. Powie was sitting on top of the dryer, waiting for her as usual.

"Hello, Powie. It's good to have someone waiting for me. It's been a long day. How about we hit the sack? Tomorrow should be interesting!"

Chapter Nine

The meteorologist on the 5 a.m. newscast said it would be cloudy with hints of sun throughout the day. There was one tiny area of sun that was peaking through the clouds as Lainey headed to the police station before seven. She drove through the drive-up at Babe's House of Caffeine, picked up a skinny Mocha Frappe for herself, and a large, hot Americano with a slice of cinnamon coffee cake for Sarge. It never hurts to bring his favorites this early in the morning.

When she walked into the station, it surprised her to see Francy sitting at the dispatch desk.

"What are you still doing here? I thought you were only working till eleven last night?"

Francy looked up and flashed a tired smile. "Deidra was supposed to come in, but her husband fell off the train at work and is in the hospital with a broken arm and leg. I'm filling in until Josey can get here to relieve me."

"That's too bad. He's been a train engineer for years. I hope he recovers quickly."

"Yeah, Deidra said he was training a new switchman and jumped down from the train to help open a switch. I guess it's about a 4-foot drop from the train ladder to the ground. The new guy didn't see him on the ground, got his foot caught in the ladder trying to jump down, and fell on him. She says he will be fine, but it will take a while to heal."

"Is Sarge in? I know I'm a little early."

"He came in a few minutes ago," Francy grinned. "Is that a peace offering or a bribe that you brought with you?"

"Whatever do you mean?" Lainey chuckled, trying to sound offended. "He works so hard, I thought he might enjoy a little bit of coffee this morning."

"Let me buzz him. I'm sure he will appreciate your kind offer!" She rang his phone and then opened the door.

"Thank you, Francy. I hope you get some rest today. You're still planning to bring supper to Pheebs this evening? Vera told me to bring potato salad."

"Yes, I am. Mom wants to ride with me since I'm bringing the barbecued pulled pork. Shep is sending a couple of pies with her. I'll see you there."

Lainey hurried down the hallway and into Sarge's office. He was standing with his back to the door, putting something into a file cabinet.

"Morning Sarge," she said gingerly. "Thanks for fitting me into your busy schedule." She walked over to his desk and sat the cup of coffee and container with the slice of cake inside on his desk. "I thought you might need a little pick-me-up this morning."

He turned around, picked up the coffee and took a long gulp. He sat it down and opened the container. "Cinnamon coffee cake, huh?" He looked at her without smiling. "And you think this will soften me up?"

"Well…yes!" She laughed and waited for his reaction. "Don't I get some credit for voluntarily coming to you instead of you summoning me?"

The captain raised his eyebrows and smiled. "That depends entirely on what you're going to ask me to do. This is about Gerry Hayward's murder, I'm sure. Have a seat and tell me what's going on."

Lainey sat down and asked about the link between Phineas Hayward and Claude Cooper before telling him about her talk with Bailee. She didn't know if his team had found out what she knew.

"When we spoke about the first envelope and Phineas Hayward being a spy for the police department, I didn't know the identity of the man killed in that raid. Has your team found out anything?"

"They have not briefed me on that. Della must have found something."

"Yes, she did. The man that was killed was Claude Cooper. That matches the second set of initials on the first scorecard." She waited for his reaction. There was none, so she continued. "He was a major bootlegger in the county and was married to Zella Brown."

That got Sarge's attention. "Zella Brown as in the Brown family that the county purchased farmland from to build Hwy 212?"

"Yep. That's the family. She died not long after Claude was killed and guess who inherited the little land and property she had left?"

"I don't know, but I'm sure you are going to fill me in."

"It was Ralph Keegler. His mother, Faye, was an aunt to Zella," she paused. "And before you ask…Ralph was Leon's father."

The captain nodded and shrugged his shoulders. "And how does this tie in with Gerry's murder?"

"I'm not sure," she admitted, "but I said if I found out who the dead man was, I would tell you. You must give me credit for that!" she teased.

"Agreed. Is that all you have to share with me? I can't believe that information alone would cause you to bring me coffee and cake," he grinned. "There has to be more."

Lainey began telling him about her conversation

with Bailee, meeting Ryan's parents, and how rude they were to her and their daughter-in-law, and about Charlie Crowfoot.

"How families treat each other is not my concern… or yours," Sarge stated. "What did you find out that I need to know?"

"Bailee informed me about Binesi's brother, Baako, who died as a teenager in an accident of some kind. Were you aware of that?"

"How is this important to our investigation?"

"Remember that Gerry had been involved in a fight over a young girl…ending in the death of another young man? You said the department would investigate the incident. Have you found out the name of the young man?"

Sarge thought for a few seconds before answering. "Apparently, you think you have."

"I can't say for sure, but what if it was Baako Ballulah? He was about the right age. That would fit into the comments Bailee overheard several times between Ryan and his father about blood revenge."

"That's jumping to a lot of conclusions," he said, shaking his head. "You're assuming a lot."

Lainey nodded and told him about her confrontation with Charlie at his bait shop the night before. The captain listened while showing no emotion.

"Vera and Shep found proof that Lois knew Gerry

and Baako in high school, and that she was more than likely dating them both. It's too much of a coincidence, don't you think?"

Sarge blinked a few times and leaned back in his chair. He was obviously thinking about how he should respond. Sitting across from him, Lainey could tell he was already aware of some, if not all, the information she had shared. Would he be willing to go with her to speak with Binesi? The silence was awkward, and she confronted him directly.

"You knew this information, didn't you? You knew about Baako and the possibility that he was the person that died in the fight with Gerry."

He nodded yes. "That still doesn't prove that Binesi murdered anyone."

"Would you go with me to speak to Binesi?"

Sarge didn't answer.

"Let me rephrase that," she said. "Would you go with me to speak with Charlie?"

Still no answer.

"If I told you that Lois Hermann had a son, would that make a difference?" She saw the surprise on his face.

"Yes, that could make a difference. Do you have proof of this?"

"Bailee found a newspaper birth record showing a baby boy born to Lois Hermann." She opened her fanny pack, took out the printout showing the notice, and handed it to him. "I don't have a name…yet."

He looked at the notice, then at his watch. "City council is meeting in a few minutes, and I am required to attend. I want to talk with you later this afternoon."

"I'm going to be at Pheebs' house this afternoon. The Whoopees are providing supper for her. Can we meet after that?"

He nodded. "Call me."

She stood up, and before leaving, asked, "What did the coroner say was the official cause of death?"

Sarge looked at her for a second before answering. "Gerry died from a hard blow to the back of his head."

"What?" she was stunned. "He was lying face up when I saw him that night. Are you thinking he was dead *before* he was caught in the machinery?"

"That is a definite possibility. I've got to get going. Call me after your visit."

Lainey left the police station and headed for the grocery store. She planned to make her mom's favorite German potato salad recipe for Pheebs and needed to buy a few ingredients. But her mind kept replaying what Sarge had told her. She kept wondering how anyone could carry a body into the bowling alley without being seen. Gerry couldn't have been dead very long when she saw him.

When she got home, she put the potatoes on to cook, then sat down at her computer to check in with her employer. She had been lucky the past few days that very few emails needed her immediate attention and today was no different. By 2 p.m., she had finished her emails, made the potato salad, and was thinking about going to see Pheebs early. There were several questions she wanted to ask her.

Lainey picked up her cell phone and said, "Hey, Siri. Call Phoebe Hayward."

The male British voice, whom she had programmed to be Siri, responded immediately. "Calling Phoebe for you."

The phone rang a few times before someone answered. "Hello, who are you wanting to speak with?"

She wasn't expecting a male voice to answer, and it startled her for a second. "I was trying to reach Phoebe Hayward. Is she there?"

"Just a minute," the man answered. She could tell he tried to muffle the sound with his hand as he talked to a woman close by. "Here she is."

"Hello? This is Phoebe Hayward. Who is this?"

"Hi, Pheebs. It's Lainey Maynard. Did I catch you at a bad time?"

"Oh. Ah, no. I can talk. I thought you were coming over around five?"

"The group is bringing supper then, but I wondered if I could come a little early. Would that be all right?"

There was a pause and again, she heard a hand

covering the phone speaker trying to muffle the sound of people talking.

"Sure. There have been visitors in and out all day. What time can I expect you?"

"Would three-thirty work?"

"Yes, that's fine. I'll see you then."

Pheebs ended the call before Lainey had a chance to say goodbye. She set her phone on the counter, wondering who the man was and why Pheebs was so abrupt. She picked up her phone again and called Della.

"Hello, Lainey. Are you still meeting us at Pheebs tonight?"

"I'm actually going over there early and wondered if you'd like to go with me."

"Sounds like something is up and you want a witness."

"You know me pretty well," she giggled into the phone. "Not a witness exactly, but a second pair of eyes and ears would be nice. Can you be ready in thirty minutes?"

"I'll be waiting. I'm bringing a fruit tray that Pheebs can put in her refrigerator. Honk when you pull into my driveway. I'll come out."

"Thanks. See you soon!"

Sure enough, Della was ready on time. She put the fruit tray on the floor in the back seat and climbed into the front passenger seat.

"Before we head over to Pheebs, tell me what's

made you suspicious? What's going on with her?" she asked Lainey.

"I have questions I wanted to ask her, and when I called to see if I could come over early, a man answered the phone."

"A man? What man? Are you sure it wasn't Gerry's voice on the answering machine?"

"No, it was not an answering machine. The guy spoke to me. And then he covered the phone while he spoke to a woman…I'm quite sure that was Pheebs."

"It could be a relative or family friend, Lainey. You know Gerry's funeral is tomorrow."

"Maybe. But I got the distinct impression both were trying to hide something," she answered, putting her car in reverse. "I'm hoping he is still there when we arrive."

Chapter Ten

The Hayward's home resembled a two-story southern plantation mansion and had been built by a wealthy banker from the Twin Cities in the early 90's. Gerry and Phoebe, knowing it needed much refurbishing and repair, had purchased it in a foreclosure sale for pennies on the dollar. It was nestled in a heavily wooded area north of Mirror Falls. The circle drive, running underneath a portico held up by white pillars, gave the illusion of grandeur from the main road.

Lainey drove through the portico, parking near the house in one of three designated spots. She and Della got out of the car, taking their food with them. As they walked to the tall front entrance, years of weather and neglect were evident over the entire structure. The pillars, paint chipped and cracked from top to bottom, were not so grand. The wooden double front doors were badly faded and a small note above the large, wrought iron doorbell button said it was out of order.

"I remember when Gerry bought this house," Della remarked as they walked up to the front door. "Larken Reneau did a radio interview with him at the time. You would have thought the Hayward's were the wealthiest people in town."

"Looks can be so deceiving. Who knew that his gambling problem would lead to all this? I understand more and more why Bailee felt such embarrassment."

Lainey knocked on the door and they waited for someone to open it. Several minutes passed before she knocked a second time…then a third time. Finally, the door creaked loudly as Pheebs opened it.

"Hello, Lainey," she greeted, then paused briefly. "Oh, I didn't know Della was coming with you. Hope you weren't waiting long. I was in the back of the house and didn't hear the knock. Come inside. We can put the food in the kitchen for now."

It was the first time either Della or Lainey had been inside the house. It was surprisingly empty of furniture and other decor. Their footsteps echoed as they followed Pheebs, walking across the marble floor, through the formal living room, and into the kitchen/dining area.

"I've been using this kitchen lately, rather than the one by the pool. It's smaller and easily accessible,"

Pheebs said, pointing to the refrigerator. "I'm sure you will find room to put your dishes."

"Thank you," Lainey answered, opening the refrigerator door. The only item inside was an open bottle of wine. She put her potato salad on a shelf and held the door while Della put her fruit tray on a different shelf.

"You'll need to excuse the house," Pheebs commented coldly. "I…we, had to sell most of the furnishings. Debt collectors don't care whether you have a chair to sit on or a bed to sleep in."

"We've not had a chance to talk with you since this happened. We're so sorry for your loss," Della said.

Pheebs nodded and without much emotion in her voice replied, "It is what it is. You mentioned you wanted to talk with me, Lainey. I have a card table with chairs in the den. Follow me." She turned and walked away from the kitchen.

Della whispered to Lainey as they followed their host. "Did you happen to notice there were two wine glasses in the sink?"

"Yes…and I swear I heard a door close when we walked into the kitchen. While I talk to Pheebs, you can look around."

The den did indeed have a card table and four chairs sitting square in the middle of the room. The three sat down and Lainey was the first to speak.

"This entire situation must be hard for you. Please

know that you do not have to discuss anything if you don't want to." She waited before continuing and, since Pheebs gave her no response, she hit the questions hard. "When did you know that Gerry was gambling heavily again?"

"Did Sarge or one of the collections agencies send you?" She was instantly defensive and angry. "I know that you are an investigator and if you've come here to put more pressure on me to pay the debts he racked up, you can leave now and take the potato salad with you. I'm not paying another dime."

"No, the collections agencies didn't send me. I lost my husband suddenly, too, and know what it's like to go through that. I'm worried about you…and Bailee."

"I'm sorry to interrupt," Della said hesitantly. "Can you tell me where the restroom is?"

"There are several so take your pick," Pheebs answered. "The closest one is down the hallway, to the left. If you get to the glass pool doors, you've gone too far."

"Thank you!" She stood up, glanced at Lainey, and left the room.

"I appreciate your concern, but I am fine. When did you speak with Bailee?"

"She told me about the envelope she found on her car the day after Gerry had received the first envelope at the bowling alley. She was scared and…"

"I know about both envelopes, and she told me that

she spoke with you." Pheebs shifted her feet under the card table. "Did she also tell you she was embarrassed by her father and his lies?"

"Yes, she did." Lainey wanted to keep her talking and distracted to give Della more time to search the house. "She mentioned arguments that she heard between you and Gerry, too."

"Oh really? And what, exactly, did Bailee tell you she heard?" Her voice was sharp, and her eyes narrowed.

"That you hated him and were tired of covering up for him."

Pheebs didn't answer. She was clinching her teeth and her cheeks were getting red. Lainey had to be careful and not push too far.

"Not to change the subject, but did you happen to talk with Chad about that first envelope? He found it in the cash register, right?"

"Are you implying that he put that envelope in the register?" She bristled and Lainey saw she hit a nerve.

"Of course not. Just wondering if you spoke with him about it."

"Chad and I don't speak that often. Gerry hired him. You saw me the night your team was practicing. I told you then that I was closing out the register. That's all. Is there anything else bothering you?"

"Did you know Bailee had a little birthday party for Ryan last night? I happened to stop by and noticed you werenn't there. Did you and Gerry approve of her marrying Ryan?" She saw Pheebs blink her eyes and stare at her. She wondered if she had pushed too hard too quickly.

"I love my daughter. Who she chose to marry is up to her. Why do you ask?"

"Bailee mentioned that she has tried very hard to fit in with Ryan's family and I was wondering how you felt about that."

"I see," she answered coyly, looking toward the door of the den. "Where's Della? It's taking her a long time to find..."

"I'm here," Della replied walking into the room. "I am sorry for the delay. My lunch didn't sit well and I'm afraid I need to go home. I'm not feeling well. Please forgive me for not staying to have dinner with you."

Pheebs looked into Della's eyes, then moved her gaze to Lainey's. It was clear that she was questioning whether to believe this sudden illness or not. She nodded and stood up.

"I certainly don't want you to feel obligated to stay here if you're sick. Let me walk both of you to the door."

"Vera and Francy will be here soon with the rest of your supper. Again, please accept my apology," Della's voice was weaker than usual. Lainey knew it was an act.

"Thank you, Pheebs, for talking with me. If you

need anything before tomorrow's service, please let me know. I'm more than happy to help you."

"I'm sure you would be," she said, her voice dripping with sarcasm. "I'm very tired and since the funeral is tomorrow, please ask your friends to drop the food off instead of staying for a while. I'm afraid I'm all chatted out this evening." She walked hurriedly to the front door, opening it without saying anything else.

"Of course. I'll let them know. You take care and we will see you tomorrow." Lainey smiled as she and Della walked outside.

Pheebs shut the door hard enough to make a slamming noise. The two friends said nothing as they walked to Lainey's car and got in. They had left the driveway and were more than a mile away from the house before either spoke.

"You'd better call Francy and let her know to drop the food off," Lainey said. "Then I want to hear what you saw or found."

Della called and explained briefly to Francy that their visit hadn't been a good one. After she ended the call, she looked at Lainey and grinned. "She wants us to come by Vera's tonight. They want to know what we did to make Pheebs mad."

"I figured that," Lainey smiled. "I know you didn't eat lunch today, so tell me what you found."

"Pheebs mentioned that if I made it to the pool area, I would have gone too far for a restroom, remember?

So, I went in the opposite direction and up the stairs. I'm sure I was over the garage. Anyway, the hallway led to a fully furnished loft apartment."

"Maybe that's where she's living until the house is sold?"

"Oh, she's living there all right. The door was open and when I stepped inside, it was one large living area. You know, with a kitchen and front room together? On the kitchen island were two more empty bottles of wine and dirty dishes were in the sink."

"Della…get to the point!"

"There was a letter on the counter from an insurance company. I started to read it when I heard someone coming down the hallway. He was talking on a cell phone to someone. I panicked and hid in the laundry room closet that was just behind the kitchen, hoping not to be discovered. It was a louvered door, and I could see as plain as day the person I heard talking…it was Chad Devon."

"Chad? That makes no sense. Pheebs said she hadn't spoken to him for several days."

"She was lying. It was Chad. Thankfully, he walked past the kitchen and sat on the couch in the front room. I could hear his side of the conversation. He was either making or confirming an appointment. And here's the biggest surprise…the appointment was with Pastor Keegler."

Lainey had pulled into Della's driveway and turned off the engine. She stared at her friend.

"Keegler? Are you sure? Why in the world would Chad be meeting with him?"

"I'm positive. Before he finished the call, I heard him thank the pastor by name, telling him *we* would see him after the funeral tomorrow. Then he got up and went into the bathroom. When I heard the shower running, I left quickly and headed back to the den where you were."

"We? Did he mean he and Pheebs or someone else?" She was silent for a moment. Thoughts, facts, and questions filled her mind. "I need to get back to my office. We're missing something key in all of this. Why don't you go to Vera's and fill them in later this evening? I'd better see Sarge this afternoon."

"I'll do that. Do you think Gerry had a life insurance policy that Chad and Pheebs are going to collect on or that they are having an affair?"

"I'm not sure. He is so much younger than she is. It's hard to believe she would be attracted to him."

"I guess you're right. Isn't he about Bailee's age?"

Lainey's eyes opened wide, and she leaned over to give her a hug. "You always say the right thing at the right time."

"Huh? I try to, I guess," she said opening the car door. "I'll be at Vera's later if you want to come by."

"See you all tomorrow at the funeral."

As she was backing out of the driveway, her cell phone rang. She knew the number was from the police station.

"Hello, this is Lainey. How can I help you?"

"I need you to come to the station immediately. I have people here waiting to speak with you," Sarge said in a very business-like manner.

"I can be there shortly. Who is waiting for me?"

"Dispatch is expecting you. Come straight to my office."

"Yes, sir." She ended the call. The drive to the station only took about five minutes, but her mind was running at least 50 mph trying to figure out who was in his office. She parked as close to the door as possible and ran inside. She didn't need to speak to the dispatcher because he buzzed open the door as soon as he saw her. She walked quickly down the hallway and stopped just short of Sarge's office door to catch her breath. Once she calmed down, she walked into the room. There were three chairs, instead of the normal two. Sarge motioned for her to sit in the chair farthest to the left. Charlie Crowfoot and Binesi Ballulah sat in the other two. Ryan was standing behind his father.

"Lainey, Mr. Crowfoot, Mr. Ballulah, and Ryan came to my office this afternoon concerning the comments you made last night to Charlie at his bait shop."

She glanced at Charlie, but he was staring directly

at Sarge. "I see. We discussed several things last evening. What comments are they speaking about?" She knew the answer before the captain spoke.

"I'll let Mr. Crowfoot tell you," he said, nodding his head at Charlie. "Go ahead."

Lainey turned in her chair enough to face him before he spoke. She noticed that Binesi was staring straight ahead, and that Ryan had his head down slightly.

Charlie took a breath, then turned to face her. "You accused our family…"

"Excuse me, Charlie, but before you say anything further, I did not accuse your family of anything," she interrupted forcefully. "I want to make sure everyone in this room is clear on that."

Binesi's face turned into a scowl. He slowly turned his chair to face Lainey's. Charlie looked at him, then to Sarge, and then to Lainey. He started to speak when Binesi held up his hand to stop him.

"I can speak for myself. Charlie has told me that you mentioned an ancient tradition known as blood revenge last night when you were speaking about Ryan's wife. I came here to make known my actions and to clear our family name."

Lainey didn't blink and her eyes never left his. She said nothing, waiting for him to continue, but Sarge intervened.

"Mr. Ballulah, this is not a trial, and no one has

accused your family of any wrongdoings. Please explain to her what you told me a few minutes ago."

The man nodded, his eyes narrowing just a bit more. "My son told me you spoke with Bailee several times and she feels that I treat her unkindly. You also came to his house last night to speak with her again." He paused, looking at her as if waiting for her to respond.

"Yes, sir. That is correct."

"Charlie also told me that you are intelligent and are aware that my younger brother, Baako, was killed years ago." Again, he paused.

"Yes, sir. That is correct." Her face was stony and expressionless. He was not going to intimidate her.

"What you may not know is that Gerry Hayward is the person who murdered…" he stopped speaking when Charlie put his hand on his arm and shook his head no. Ryan put his hand on his father's shoulder. After a few seconds, Binesi continued. "Gerry Hayward was responsible for my brother's death. Did I want revenge for this? Yes. It is tradition that someone pay for taking a life." His voice cracked and for a moment, it sounded like he might break down. He quickly regained the strength in his voice and continued speaking. "In this day and time, it is no longer a life for a life. But some type of compensation is due for the family's loss." He took a deep breath and turned his face back toward the captain. He was finished speaking.

Charlie patted Binesi's arm before removing his hand. He turned to face Lainey once more.

"I do have a heart, even though you may think otherwise," he began. "You reminded me that Bailee is the innocent bystander here and not at fault. I couldn't sleep last night and this morning, I went to Binesi and Ryan. That's why we are here."

"Uncle Charlie, let me explain." Ryan's voice caught both his father and Charlie off guard. They were not expecting him to speak. "It's true. When my father found out that I was dating Bailee Hayward, in his mind, he had found a way to get compensation for Baako's death." He paused as tears filled his eyes. "I was to marry her, and then our family would reject her. The hurt she felt was meant to make Gerry suffer. That would be compensation for the pain he had caused my family. I love my father, my family…and I do care for Bailee." He couldn't hold the tears back any longer and he began sobbing.

Binesi sat stone faced. He didn't reach out to console his son nor did he try to speak in his defense. He sat in silence. Charlie got up, walked over to Ryan, and hugged him. When he had stopped crying, Charlie sat back down and spoke to Sarge.

"Our family would not commit murder. And as far as that envelope that was given to Bailee, we have no idea where it came from. I hope you see that we are telling the truth."

Sarge nodded. "If you have nothing else to add, I appreciate your coming in." He looked at Lainey, who sat quietly, processing what she had just heard.

Binesi stood up, gave a slight bow to the captain, and walked out the office door. Ryan followed behind him.

"Thank you both," Charlie said, standing up. "You may not agree with traditions, but I hope this clears the air about any idea that the Ballulah's had anything to do with Gerry's murder." He extended his hand to the captain.

Sarge stood up to shake his hand. "Thank you for coming in."

Charlie turned to walk out the door and nodded to Lainey. She nodded in return. Once he left the room, Sarge walked to the door and closed it. He walked back to his desk, sat in his chair, and waited for Lainey to speak, wondering what she would say. He let her sit for several minutes before he broke the silence.

"Looks like you were correct about Baako and Gerry. There isn't any legal action for me to take. What are you thinking?"

"I feel for Bailee, and I hope that Ryan will be honest with her. But this opens more questions about who was behind the envelope."

"I agree." He opened one of the drawers in his desk,

took out a piece of paper and handed it to Lainey. "Now would be a good time to show you this."

She took the paper, read it, then read it again. "Lois died from pneumoconiosis? Isn't that called black lung disease? How did you find out?"

"Della's not the only person who has resources," he smiled. "She had gone to work in a coal mine on the night shift to try and support her son. Even though she didn't go down into the mine, she was exposed to the coal dust. When she was too sick to work, she asked an older couple to care for her child. We haven't found the names of that couple yet."

Lainey sat forward in her chair. "What about her parents? Did they know she had a son?"

"It's doubtful. Once Lois left Mirror Falls, her parents didn't hear from her again, until they were notified that she had died."

"This is a long shot, but do you know who the father of the boy was?"

Sarge shook his head. "No. Unless we find the people who raised him or find his original birth name, there is no way to tell."

"Have you spoken with Pheebs lately?"

"I thought you were going to take supper to her this evening. No, I haven't. Pastor Leon said he would contact me if they needed something."

"Yeah…" her voice drifted off. "His name keeps popping up in places, doesn't it?"

"Hold on," the captain said, his smile turning into a frown. "What makes you say that?"

She grinned and tried to change the subject. "No special reason. I need to be going. Is there anything else you need from me?"

He wrinkled his mouth and gazed at her for a moment. "Only if you have more to tell me."

"Nope. I'm all chatted out as Pheebs would say." She laughed.

"I'm missing the joke here. What?"

Lainey stood. "Are you going to the funeral?"

"I don't think so. Several officers are and I told them I'd cover."

She nodded. "I'll know where to find you if I need you." She winked, turned, and walked out of his office.

Chapter Eleven

The wind had picked up and grey clouds threatened to open their flood gates once more. Leaving the station parking lot, Lainey decided to drive by the First Methodist Church. Gerry's funeral was to be held there tomorrow and she had a strong hunch that the church office might still be open.

Mirror Falls was like many small towns. While it didn't have multi-lane freeways, rush hour traffic jams, or major sports arenas, it had no shortages of banks, bars, and churches. There was at least one of the three institutions on every street corner. Lainey smiled as she pulled into the church's parking lot. The tall, red brick church, its white bell tower and pointed steeple reaching high into the sky, reminded her of the church she grew up attending.

She recognized one of the other two cars in the parking lot. It was Paul Kristiansen's funeral home van. She got out of her car, hurried up the concrete steps to the church entrance, and tugged open the heavy wooden door. She hoped to find Paul inside finalizing details for the next day. Instead, she found herself facing Pastor Leon in the foyer.

"Hello," he said softly. "Are you needing something? The church office is closed, but..." he stopped after realizing who she was. "Oh, it's you, Lainey. I didn't recognize you. What can I do for you?" His voice had gotten louder...and stronger.

"Hello, Pastor," she answered, holding out her hand to greet him. She wanted to see if his handshake was as weak as it was in Sarge's office the other day. It wasn't. "I noticed Paul's van here and wondered if I could talk with him."

"Paul's not here, but one of his employees is setting up the viewing room for tomorrow's service. We're expecting a large crowd to attend."

A lightning bolt flashed, followed by a loud clap of thunder at the same time as he finished speaking. Lainey's first thought was that someone above was either warning him to watch what he said or warning her to keep her guard up. She worked hard to keep from smiling.

"Perhaps I can talk with you instead. I realize you're busy, but do you have a few minutes to spare for me?" She could hear the rain pounding on the roof.

"I am busy, but we can chat until the hard rain stops. Let's move to my office. It's the room behind the altar."

She followed him through the sanctuary, up the few stairs to the altar area, and through a door to the left. She kept thinking it was odd that he used the word 'chat.' He turned on the lights and she was surprised how large the room was. It was very modern, complete with cherry wood bookshelves and a matching ornate desk. A leather couch and coffee table sat beneath an arched-framed stained-glass window. A cabinet with a wet bar was directly across from the office door. A bottle of Mogen David wine was sitting out. A small refrigerator was inside the cabinet below the sink.

"Let's sit on the couch, shall we? Would you like a bottle of water or Coke?" he asked as she sat down.

"No, thank you. This is a nice office."

"My congregation has been extremely kind to me." He walked over to the refrigerator, took out a bottle of water, and then sat down on the opposite end of the couch. "Tell me, Lainey," he twisted off the bottle cap and took a drink. "What is bothering you?"

"Oh, I'm not here for counseling," she began, knowing he knew she wasn't either. "I understand you've been counseling Bailee and Phoebe."

She watched as he took another sip of water. His

friendly smile slowly turning into a suspicious smirk. "Such a tragic situation. Facing foreclosure on their business and home…and now the murder of poor Gerry. Yes, I've been helping them as much as possible."

"You've known them a long time. I'm sure Phoebe appreciates your kindness." She noticed a slight squint in his eyes.

"The Haywards are long time members here."

"Didn't you attend high school with Gerry and Phoebe?"

Before he could answer, a young man knocked on his door. It was Paul's employee, Todd.

"Sorry to bother you, Pastor, but do you have keys to the upstairs storage room? Mr. Kristiansen said the plant stands and easels that we use for services are stored there. I'd like to get them setup tonight if possible."

"Of course, Todd," he replied. "Give me one second."

"No problem. I'll wait in the hallway for you."

Pastor Keegler nodded, then stood up. "Excuse me, Lainey. This shouldn't take too long."

She watched him leave the room, and when she couldn't hear their footsteps or voices, she quickly began searching through his desk. The drawers weren't locked and contained nothing out of the ordinary. Looking around the room, she focused on the wet bar cabinet and its few drawers. She found only communion supplies. Disappointed, she turned to walk back to the couch, looking around the room for anything she had missed. Not noticing the small throw rug in front of the wet bar, she tripped on one of its edges and fell hard on the wooden floor.

"Ouch," she said aloud. "Way to go, Lainey, klutzy as ever." Putting her hands on the floor to get up, she noticed a couple of the boards bent when she put pressure on them. She stood up, glanced at the door, then stepped on the same boards. They bowed under her feet. Grabbing a pen from the desktop, she pried up the boards carefully. Underneath was a white gift box, like the ones used to wrap Christmas presents. She opened it, took out the contents, and quickly replaced the boards. Not having much time, she took the pen and, using a neon green sticky note on the desk, wrote a note that she had to leave.

She walked briskly out of the office, down the sanctuary's middle aisle, and was feet away from the front entrance when she heard Keegler's voice.

"You're leaving rather suddenly, aren't you?" He was walking through the sanctuary toward her.

Not stopping, she raised her hand to wave and shouted, "Sorry! I've been called away." She opened the large church door and ran to her car. Once inside, she locked the doors, started the car, and headed back toward the police station. Keegler was standing in the parking lot getting drenched by rain. He watched her drive away.

"Siri, call Sarge!" she commanded loudly. She knew Leon would quickly realize she had taken the items from the floor and Sarge's office was the safest place she knew.

"Calling Sarge," her British man answered.

The phone rang several times while Lainey sped toward the station. She had parked and was hurrying to the main door when Sarge finally picked up.

"I was on my way home. What is it this time?" he asked.

"I'm at dispatch...let me in!"

He knew by the sound of her voice that something was terribly wrong. The lady sitting at dispatch looked bewildered, but buzzed the door open immediately. Lainey ran in, looking behind her worried that someone had followed. She turned her head back just in time to feel Sarge's badge hit her in the face. She groaned, grabbed her nose, and jerked backward, dropping everything she was carrying. After hearing the urgency in her voice, the captain hurried from his office to meet her. The two collided hard at the door and Lainey took the brunt of the hit. Her nose was bleeding profusely.

"Sally, grab the first aid kit and come to my office," Sarge ordered. He took Lainey by the arm and said, "Come on, let's get your nose fixed up." The two walked slowly to his office. Sally was waiting with the first aid kit as ordered. "Here you go, Sarge. Should I call Bart? He's the EMT on call tonight," she asked.

"No, we've got this. Thank you, Sally."

"No problem." She nodded and left his office.

Sarge looked at Lainey and handed her several tissues. "Take your fingers and squeeze your nostrils together," he instructed. "It'll take a few minutes before the bleeding stops."

She rolled her eyes at him. "I've had nose bleeds before," she snapped and then thought she'd better apologize. "Sorry. I didn't see you in the doorway."

He smiled, then noticed her elbow was skinned. He grabbed it and shook his head. "How did this happen? You didn't fall in my office."

Again, she rolled her eyes and tried to speak, but her voice came out sounding like Alvin the chipmunk. "It's hard to talk with my nose plugged!"

Sarge sighed and then chuckled. "Okay, okay. Sit still. I'm going to clean up the mess you made in my hallway. We can talk afterward."

"Wait…the things I dropped…" her eyes had widened, and she still sounded silly.

"Don't worry. I'll bring everything to my office."

Lainey sat, holding her nose, and putting her thoughts together for the next twenty minutes or so. She hadn't had a chance to look through the items she found in Keegler's office, but she had caught a glimpse of a photo of Lois. She was thinking and mumbling to herself when Sarge walked back in. She let go of her nose and waited to see if the bleeding had stopped. It had. She didn't dare rub it or her face for a while longer.

"Good," the captain said to her. "Looks like the bleeding has stopped."

"Yes, but my face is sore."

He laid the items Lainey had dropped on his desk, arranging them to face her. Then he sat down in the chair beside her, looking at her face. "You're going to have a story to tell. Looks like you're going to have quite a bruise under your right eye." He smiled. "We used to call those 'shiners' when we arrested prisoners who had been fighting."

"I'm going to tell people you tortured me," she replied, trying to be funny. "I'd laugh, but it makes my cheek hurt!"

"Seriously, you left my office not two hours ago. Give me the details. Where/what/who…and why you were scared."

She straightened her shoulders, trying to look calm. "I wasn't frightened. I was hurrying here to show those." She pointed to the things on his desk, then leaned forward to look more closely.

"Before we talk about those items," Sarge cautioned her, "tell me what you did when you left my office earlier."

Lainey sat back in the chair, rubbed her forehead

gently, and began explaining about her visit with Pheebs, finding Chad at the house, and about the insurance letter that Della saw. She was going to continue when he stopped her.

"Let me understand fully," he stated. "While you were feeling out Pheebs, Della was playing detective and found Chad living in an upstairs loft?"

"I wasn't feeling Pheebs out, but yes. Della saw Chad and he was living in an upstairs loft."

"And what about the insurance letter?"

She blew out a breath as if she were blowing out birthday cake candles. "The loft was not locked, so Della went inside. On the counter she saw bottles of wine and a letter that appeared to come from an insurance company. Before she could read the letter, Chad returned to the loft."

One side of the captain's mouth twisted upward. "She hid in the room, right? Do you realize what could have happened if she had been seen?"

She nodded yes. "She heard Chad talking on his cell phone, confirming an appointment for him and Pheebs with Pastor Keegler for tomorrow after the funeral. Then she came back downstairs, and we left the house. That's when you called, and I came here." She waited for him to respond. When he didn't, she continued. "I can't prove this, but it's evident that Chad is living with Pheebs…either as a guest or they are having an affair. I don't really believe it's the latter. She's old enough to be his mother."

"That happens all the time. What makes you so sure they are not seeing each other?"

"My gut, I guess. Sarge, you're going to think I'm crazy, but what if Chad was blackmailing Pheebs and Gerry?"

He sat silently, tapping his fingers on the arm of his chair. Then, as if he decided to trust her, he mentioned that Shep had been by to see him that morning.

"He showed me the pictures he and Vera found from the library. Lois, Gerry, Baako, and Keegler made quite a quartet, didn't they?"

She didn't answer immediately. In her mind, puzzle pieces were finally beginning to set in place, and she wanted to have her ducks in a row before saying anything. Her head was beginning to throb, and she asked Sarge if he could get her something to drink. He nodded, walked out of room, and came back quickly with a cup of water. Too quickly for her to look at the papers on his desk.

"I've got Tylenol if you need," he said, handing her the water.

"No, thanks. I'll be okay," she answered, taking a long sip of the cool liquid. "There's more you need to know."

"I'm listening."

"When I left your office this afternoon, I drove over

to First Methodist. I thought the church would be open and I could look around."

"Look around in Keegler's office, you mean."

She cringed and a lightning bolt of guilt ran through her. "Yes…" She hated that he knew her so well. "I saw Kristiansen's van parked in front and thought Paul would be setting up for tomorrow's service. Instead of Paul, I ran into Keegler."

"I see. Did you manage to get inside his office?" He questioned, although he already knew the answer.

"You know I did. While we were talking, he had to leave the office for a few minutes…so I looked around and didn't find anything."

The scowl on his face showed he didn't believe her. "You're telling me you found nothing."

"Until I fell on the floor, I hadn't found anything."

"What? How did you fall? Did he push you?"

"No, no…nothing like that," she smiled. "There was a throw rug on the floor, and I tripped on the edge of it, skinning my elbow. That's when I found that the floor had two loose boards." She cut her eyes to the items that were sitting on the captain's desk. "Those items were underneath the boards. I took them, and tried to leave before Keegler came back. But he saw me as I was going out of the church entrance. I drove here as fast as possible. That's why I was running when you hit me." She grinned.

"I didn't hit you!" He kidded. "You'd have two shiners if I had punched you."

"Can I please look at these now?" she asked, almost begging. "I'm sure you examined them when you picked them up."

He nodded. "Yes, I did go through them. Take your time checking them out." There was something in his face that made Lainey realize he wasn't sharing everything he knew. Take her time checking them out? He would never say that…unless.

"Do you know who murdered Gerry?" she asked abruptly. "I'm guessing I don't need to look at these items, do I?"

His pager beeped and Sally from dispatch was summoning him. "Sarge, please come to the intake room. The person of interest you wanted picked up is here."

"I'm on my way." He stood up, pointed at the papers, and said, "I'm closing my office door. Read these and do not come out until I come to get you." He started to leave the room, then hit his pager. "Sally, please have O'Riley come to my office. I want to make sure no one comes or goes out of it for now."

"Really, Sarge? Do you think that is necessary? I'll stay here, I promise."

He smiled and walked out, closing the door behind him. She heard him tell the deputy to make sure no one enters or leaves his office till he returned.

"Well, that's a fine how-do-you-do," she grumbled aloud. Then she smiled. She knew he was thinking of her safety. She focused on the papers on the desk. There were several items, and she picked up the red envelope that had first caught her eye when she was in Keegler's office. It was never meant to be mailed. The front had one word written on it. Lois. The ink had faded, and she turned it over gently. The crease on the top of the envelope showed signs of wear and tear. Someone had opened and closed this many times over the years. Carefully she took out the yellowed stationery and read it silently.

My dearest Lois,

How many times over the past five years have I asked you to marry me? And each time you tell me that it is not the right time. You know I have loved you since our school days. When you left Mirror Falls, I was lost without you. I gave up college and my family to search for you. The day I learned you were in Fargo, my heart leaped with joy! I moved here to find you. Remember how I hugged you the first time? I can still feel it.

When you told me about your boy, Chad, and that Gerry was the father, I said then and I will say it now...it doesn't matter. I love you and will raise little Chad as my own. Please, my love, marry me. It is torture seeing you every night at work and not being able to hug you or kiss you.

How much longer will you keep me waiting? We will be so happy if you marry me! I saw your eyes this morning as the shift ended and I know you are tired. If you are not feeling well, let me take care of you. You are not and will never be a burden to me. I will protect you and fight anyone who tries to harm you until I take my last breath. You are my life, my future, and I love you. Leon

Lainey folded the letter, placed it back in the envelope, and sat it down on the desk. She wanted to feel sorry for Leon, but she couldn't. She picked up two old polaroid snapshots. One was a vibrant, happy, and beautiful young Lois. The other told a different story. Lois, looking much older, thinner, and tired, was sitting in a chair holding a curly headed little boy. He was wearing a birthday hat with the number 5 on it.

Placing the photos back on the desk, she picked the three papers that were left. She was surprised to see that the first one was a copy of the same article Della had found talking about the police raid from years ago. Someone had drawn an arrow pointing to the back side of the paper. She turned it over and swallowed hard. There were three sentences handwritten on the page.

Phineas Hayward was responsible for Great Uncle Claude's death.

We should have owned all the land and gotten the money for selling it.

My dad died trying to get that money back.

Lainey put the second page on top of the article and began reading. It was typed on an old manual typewriter using a black ribbon. The letters weren't uniform, some were darker than others. It was a legal notice and was addressed to the family of Baako Ballulah.

Our investigation into the unfortunate death of your son, Baako, is complete. We have not found evidence to support your claim that he was murdered. The coroner's final report shows that he bled to death when his arm was severed in an unfortunate accident.

Our department extends their deepest condolences for your loss. Please let us know if we can be of service to you or your family.

She put the two pages back on the captain's desk before looking through the last paper. Her thoughts went back to the first conversation with Sarge. At that time, he warned her that the murderer could have planned this for years. It looked like Leon had done just that.

As damaging as the other evidence was, the final paper sealed the Pastor's fate. It was a letter written to Leon from Phoebe Hayward, and it was dated only a few months ago. She read the letter aloud.

Leon,

I can't say I'm happy that you told me that Chad Devon is the illegitimate son of Gerry and some girl named Lois. However, given the history of my lying husband, I don't doubt that it is true. You realize my financial situation and

I'm appalled that you suggested I give you money or you would tell the community this news.

I've already spoken with Chad, making him aware of this. Together, we have come up with a solution that we feel would not only satisfy your request but appease my hatred and contempt for Gerry.

I will make sure that Gerry knows about Chad, and I will make sure he hires him to work at the bowling alley. You mentioned that you were going to head up a fundraiser to help us pay off the enormous gambling debts he racked up, hopefully ensuring we can keep the house. I doubt seriously that you really care one way or the other, but since you are trying to squeeze money from me, here is my proposition.

Hold the fundraiser as planned. We both know it will not be enough to pay off all debts. Since you oversee the funds, you can under-report the amount that is brought in. Gerry's been cooking the books for years, so I know it can be done. I suggest we split the difference between us. I'll make sure Chad is compensated in some way.

If you don't agree, I will go to the police. Whether they believe me or not doesn't matter. At this point, I have nothing more to lose.

Chapter Twelve

Lainey heard the captain's voice before he opened the office door. She put the letter she had been reading back on the desk as he walked in and sat down.

"Your expression tells me you've read these items. I can't accuse you of breaking and entering to steal these…" he cleared his throat, then added, "and I can't accuse you of stealing these since you accidentally came across those loose boards." He leaned back in his chair, and he was not smiling. "And it's doubtful they can be used as evidence of any kind. So, what do you suggest we do now?"

What? He's asking me what to do next? My brain is still overloaded! She shrugged her shoulders and looked at him, then stalled to gather her thoughts.

"I would think that the information we had

previously, the envelopes and now this new information sitting on your desk, would be enough to at least talk with Keegler. Don't you?"

He nodded for a moment, then leaned forward in his chair. His eyes focused on her face. She figured he was going to chew her out for going to Keegler's office in the first place. Instead, he asked if her face and head were still hurting.

"My face is sore, but my head feels better if I don't make any fast movements." She answered, confused by his question. "Are you going to speak with Keegler after the funeral?"

"No," his answer was short and direct. The office phone rang and he answered it. "This is Sarge." He was still looking directly at her bruised face. "Thank you. Please send it in." He hung up the phone and smiled but said nothing.

She heard footsteps and turned to see Deputy O'Riley coming into the office. He was carrying a Starbuck's coffee cup.

"One skinny, large Mocha Frappe as you requested, sir." He sat the cup on the captain's desk in front of her. She looked at Sarge and smiled.

"Thank you, Deputy," he replied, watching as Lainey took a drink through the cup's straw.

"This is very kind of you," she said between sips. "I really needed this."

He grinned. "To expand on my answer to your

question, I won't be talking with Pastor Keegler tomorrow because I've already booked him tonight on the suspicion of murder."

"What? When? You mean he's here, now?"

"By the time I went to the front to pick up after your fall, Sally had already cleared the area. She handed me these and once I read them, I issued a warrant for his immediate arrest. He was the person of interest who was picked up about an hour ago."

"So you *do* think this was enough evidence!" She grinned so widely, she winced a little and touched her cheek below her eye. "Ouch. That is going to be sore for a while."

Sarge chuckled loudly and again, sat back in his chair. "Keegler was brought in and before I could question him, he waived his right to an attorney and confessed that he murdered Gerry Hayward."

"Wow, I'm stunned. He must have spent years planning to get Gerry," she said shaking her head. "To confess so quickly and waiving his right to an attorney sounds fishy to me. Doesn't it to you?"

"I've seen this many times. Keegler began rambling about finally being able to see Lois again. We were recording his interview and I reminded him that insanity pleas, while they worked on television shows, would not work in his case. I may have mentioned that Phoebe and Chad were willing to testify against him and he should speak to an attorney."

"Ah. Good thinking. What did he do then?"

"Like a miracle, his sanity returned, and he requested the district attorney visit with him. Kerry Garrett is with him now."

She smiled and finished her Mocha Frappe. "When he confessed, did he say how he killed Gerry?"

The captain nodded and began explaining that Leon sent the envelopes not only to scare Gerry, but to move suspicion away from himself to the Ballulahs and Chad. Since he knew that Gerry murdered Baako, he decided the best way to carry out his revenge was to kill him in the same way. That would imply at least one of the Ballulahs was involved. Leon was also aware that Gerry was closing the alley early that evening to get the machines ready. He had a key to the alley, so it was easy for him to get in and get out without being seen.

He walked to the back and found Gerry bending over one of the machines, oiling it. Leon picked up a spare bowling ball and hit him from behind. The blow killed him instantly. To make the threats on the scorecards more real, he moved Gerry's body to lane 4 and shut down the machines. He realized, once he said to turn them on to start the tournament, Gerry's arm would be caught in the gears.

"What about Pheebs? Why would he try to extort her? He knew they had no money," she asked.

"I'm going to talk with Phoebe and Chad tomorrow

afternoon. You mentioned that Della saw a letter from an insurance company, correct?"

"You think there is a life insurance policy and Leon knew about it?"

"That wouldn't surprise me. But until I talk with them tomorrow, it is merely speculation."

Lainey paused for a second, wondering if she should ask if charges might be filed against Pheebs or Chad. "Is there a chance that charges…" she was interrupted by a familiar voice shouting in the hallway.

"The captain sent for me, young lady. Now let me inside!" Vera demanded, walking past Sally at the dispatch desk into Sarge's office. "Oh, my dear. You look simply awful!"

Lainey stood up as her friend ran to hug her. "I'm okay, no need to worry," she smiled, trying to calm Vera, who had tears in her eyes. "Did you drive here in this storm?"

"Nope," Francy answered, walking into the room. Della and Shep followed closely behind her. "When Sarge called me, he said bring the lady cat burglar, the house snooper, and his favorite chef. So here we are, and we need a hug!"

The captain watched as the friends hugged Lainey and commented on her bruises. He was not expecting Vera to walk around the desk and order him to stand up.

"Sarge, I'm giving you a hug whether you like it or

not!" She gave him the biggest bear hug he'd had in a while.

"Thank you, Vera. I knew Lainey needed her friends this evening and I was glad to help."

"Is that the only reason you called?" Vera sounded a little disappointed. "Francy said you wanted me to bring my strawberry rhubarb bars. There's a fresh batch at the front desk!"

The group laughed and talked for a couple more minutes before Sarge interrupted them.

"I'm sure you all want to know what has happened. She can fill you in, but not in my office. Take her home, please...I've had enough Lainey-sitting for one night!" He smiled. "And I'm taking those bars home with me."

Murder in the Backwater Preview

Two Months ago

Lainey Maynard had been licking stamps for more than an hour. "My tongue is so dry, it's sticking to the roof of my mouth!"

Francy dropped the ink pen she was holding and rubbed the fingers on her right hand. "You think that's bad? My hand is cramped into a permanent claw from addressing these envelopes."

"You both volunteered to help me," Della reminded them. "I told you I had some mailings to do."

"Some mailings? This is the third batch! We must be close to a thousand," Francy said.

"Twelve hundred to be exact," Della grinned.

Lainey and Francy groaned at the same time.

"I'll make a pot of coffee," Vera said. "And I've got sugar cookies fresh from the oven."

Della smiled and looked at the stacks of letters in front of her. "Why does Mirror Falls have to mail out these notices for the Governor's office? He's the Governor, for Pete's sake. I'm sure he has a budget for postage!"

"It's not some fishing weekend," Francy replied. "It's the official start of the fishing season. It's a big deal to have it in Mirror Falls."

"Paul says it brings a ton of tourists to town… and they spend money," Della said.

Francy leaned back in her chair. "It's political. Don't let anyone tell you it is anything else."

Vera brought the coffee pot to the table and poured a cup for each of the girls. "It's been that way since I can remember."

"Fishing and politics," Lainey mused. "Seems like odd bedfellows."

"Every news station in the state will have reporters here. Sarge will put all his officers on duty for that night," Francy said. "Things can get out of hand quickly."

"I remember," Vera nodded. "Doc planned on being called to the emergency room at least three times that first night."

"People get hurt fishing?" Della asked.

"Sure they do. Dad took fish hooks out of cheeks, ears, and hands. Do you know where the most injuries occur?" Francy questioned.

"In the Governor's boat," Vera stated. "Those darn politicians have a quick temper!"

Lainey shrugged her shoulders. "Grown men fighting over the size of fish they caught?"

"Oh, they're catching a lot more than fish," Francy grimaced. "You'll see."

Vera glanced at Francy and then at Lainey. "Honey, you have no idea how much trouble hosting the fishing opener is going to be. Mirror Falls might never be the same."

Goosebumps suddenly covered Lainey's arms and she felt a little nauseous.

Something's going to happen. I can feel it. Do I dare tell them?

For six months of the year, Mirror Falls transforms from a popular tourist vacation destination for boaters, campers, bikers, hikers, and baseball fans, into a deserted ghost town.

Old Man Winter's frigid winds, below zero temperatures, and mountains of snow force each resident into hibernation. The days when the grey sky gods allowed the sun to briefly peek its head out from among the dreary clouds could be counted on one hand. The past winter had been unusually long and bitter with more than 90 inches of the white stuff falling from October through late March.

Cabin Fever, as the locals called it, gripped every member of every household. Dogs, cats, and hamsters in town had it, too. The fever showed no mercy. Even houses felt its wrath.

Utility rooms and mud rooms were cluttered with piles of heavy down-filled coats, plaid woolen scarfs, hats and gloves, and well-worn snow boats covered with salt stains from the months of residue left on the roads. Scarred snow shovels and tired snowblowers stood in reverent silence by the garage doors, ready for action again on a moment's notice.

By the time April arrived, Cabin Fever had transformed the kindest, most even tempered of the locals into angry, impatient, caged animals chomping at the bit to escape the confines of their homes. Conversation at the local coffee shops revolved around one topic… the Minnesota Governor's Fishing Opener. It was the annual affair that kept hopes alive and locals from killing each other during the long winter.

"It's Cabin Fever, I tell you," Shep Morton said as he handed Vera the takeout food she'd ordered. "I'm getting sick and tired of cranky customers."

Vera frowned at his remark and nodded. "Oh, I know all about that. Doc referred to it as GBS… Grumpy Blues Syndrome."

"I bet he saw a bunch of angry and depressed patients. They're all crazy."

"A few of them thought he was Dear Abby! He'd have perfectly healthy patients come in and expect him to sit and listen to their complaints."

"Gossip central, that's what Doc's office was. Bet he had stories to tell you."

She picked up her box and turned to leave. Stopping short of the restaurant door, she turned and looked back.

"Are *you* still feuding with Charlie at the Bait Shop?"

He squinted his eyes in her direction.

"The supply committee voted to buy all the bait from him this year."

Shep set his jaw and stared out the window.

"The last food committee meeting is tonight. See you there," she grinned, opened the door, and made sure it slammed shut behind her.

"Darned old goat!" she said aloud as she got into her car. "How Sally ever put up with him is beyond me."

The Whoopee group decided to meet this week at Francy's house instead of going out to one of the regular eating spots. With only a week left before the fishing opener, each was on at least one committee and needed to spend time working on various tasks. Vera had volunteered to pick up something for dinner and the ladies were sitting at the dining room table waiting for her.

Francy looked down at her watch. "Mom said she'd be here no later than 5:30. It's already 6:15. I apologize that she's late, again."

"Wasn't she going to pick up supper from the Backwater?" Lainey asked.

"Yes, and I'll bet she and Shep are wasting time arguing about something or other."

Lainey and Della looked at each other and grinned.

"What's the story, Francy?" Della asked. "Spill the beans."

"It's a ridiculous ongoing feud that started when Shep and Charlie bowled on the same team."

"Bowling?" Lainey couldn't help smiling. "In a bowling league?"

Della rested her elbows on the table. "Paul said bowling was a *big deal* back in the day."

"It was. During the winter, bowling alleys were the only places open. All of the towns around Mirror Falls had leagues and hosted tournaments," Francy stated. "Women's leagues, men's leagues, mixed leagues… anything that could stand on two legs and manage to throw a bowling ball down the alley joined a league."

Lainey shook her head in amazement. "I've never heard of a bowling feud lasting fifty years. What did they argue over?"

Francy looked at the wrinkled tablecloth and grinned.

"Does Vera know, Francy?" Della asked.

"Dad might have told her."

Lainey caught the sly look between the two.

"All right. Tell me what happened," she demanded.

The doorbell rang and Francy got up to answer it. Vera came inside, apologizing for being late.

"Hi, girls," she stated, handing the food to Francy then taking off her shoes and coat. "I've got comfort food... meatloaf, mashed potatoes, and gravy!"

The conversation during dinner was light and revolved around the upcoming event.

"It's your first time serving on the host board, Lainey. Is it awkward having Raymond as the chairman?" Della asked.

"You don't have to answer that, sweetie," Vera quickly chimed in. "We know it's hard for you."

Lainey twisted a piece of the tablecloth in her hands. She could feel her face flush and her entire body felt like she was in a sauna. Raymond Sullivan, the handsome CEO of the Sullivan's Best Poultry empire, had unexpectedly swept her off her feet. She hadn't dared become involved with anyone since she lost her husband. They had dated for a few months and she was happy. Until the day he called to inform her it was over.

His voice had been cold and distant. His words sharp and business like. "Lainey, you're a beautiful woman and I enjoy spending time with you. But I'm not ready for a serious relationship..."

She shivered at the memory of his voice, then tried to regain her composure.

"I don't have much contact with him," she shrugged her shoulders. "He doesn't attend many of the meetings."

"In my day, men were polite and respectful. If they needed to talk with you, they came to your house - face to face." Vera stated. "None of this face calling or face texting or whatever it is now."

Chuckling, Francy replied, "Mom, cell phones hadn't been invented when you were dating. Guys had to find a pay phone to call you back then. And it's FaceTime, not face calling."

"We had a home phone. Besides, who had a quarter for a pay phone?" Vera asked. "Are you okay, Lainey? I'm sure he hurt your feelings."

"I'm fine working on the committee. Raymond Sullivan is past history."

How I wish I were over him!

A quiet minute passed before Della broke the silence.

"The registration committee let me be the lead contact."

"You mean you got the short end of the straw when it came time to pick a chairman," Francy laughed out loud.

"Anyway," Della continued, trying hard not to smile, "I think we have five hundred entries so far. We've planned for at least twelve hundred."

"I've been studying up for the trivia contest again," Vera added. "I'm going to win that Mexico vacation package this year."

"What about Faye?" Della kidded. "Hasn't she

beaten you the last several years?"

"She broke her hip in February and moved to Florida to live with her kids," Francy grimaced. "Of course you'll beat her, Mom."

"Well, you never know. She could send in an absentee ballot!"

The laughter that followed lightened the mood and Lainey was thankful for that. She didn't want to think about Raymond.

"I do have a dilemma," Della said. "Paul tells me that the opener is politically motivated. I'm having a difficult time trying to organize who is sitting in the boat with the Governor. Any ideas?"

Francy sighed. "Politically motivated is an understatement. It's all about politics… and money."

"How so?" Lainey piped in. "Money for the city, I can see. But what makes it benefit the Governor?"

"There are only two reasons to have an official fishing opener," Vera began. "The first is for local politicians to bend the Governor's ear and get special funds for their own interests. The second is a campaign photo opportunity for his re-election bid."

"Yep. All the major news stations will follow him like a hawk," Francy agreed. "It's ridiculous the amount of dollars spent protecting the Governor so news anchors can take his picture in front of a bar holding a Minnesota craft beer."

"Channel Ten kept showing a video of him sitting

behind the wheel of a big ol' green John Deere tractor last year. The wind kept blowing his straw hat off!" Della laughed loudly. "He'd pick it up, try to pose, then it would fly off again."

Lainey rubbed her eyebrow and wrinkled her nose. "I thought it was to start the official fishing season in Minnesota."

"Oh, it is. But remember, we have more than 1.4 million licensed anglers in our state. Out of that, more than five hundred thousand will fish on opening day. And we have eighteen thousand miles of fishing streams and waters," Vera commented.

"You sound like a World Book Encyclopedia," Francy added, rolling her eyes.

"It's all in the trivia study guide. I told you, I'm going to win this year!"

"Back to my question, please," Della directed. "Whom should I put in the boat with the Governor? Can I put Democrats and Republicans in the same boat?"

Francy cleared her throat and sat up straight in her chair. "No! Only his party members in his boat. The opposing party is in the boat just behind him."

"Paul cautioned me to do that as well," Della answered.

Lainey thought she was joking. "Seriously? It's that important to keep them separate? It's just fishing, for Pete's sake."

Francy closed her eyes and nodded. "Fishing has nothing to do with."

"Years ago, Doc was in charge of the Governor's boat. Months prior to the opener, people took him out to lunch, bought him gifts, gave him tickets to sports games. They tried to bribe him to put them in the boat."

"How did he decide who got in?" Della asked.

"He put all the names in a bag, shook them up, and drew out six names."

"Well, I guess that's fair. Maybe I'll try that."

"Tell her the rest of the story, Mom."

Vera took a deep breath, then rolled her eyes. "The six whose names were drawn were happy. But twelve of those whose names weren't drawn, were terribly angry. They demanded to know how he made the decision and accused him of showing partiality. When he told them he drew names out of a bag, they accused him of cheating. They demanded he hold a public drawing with the news channels present."

Della shook her head in disbelief. "That's unbelievable. What did Doc do?"

"He told them to go jump in the lake, waders and all," Vera grinned.

Lainey chuckled.

"I think he later regretted his choice of words. Those twelve started a smear campaign. They spread rumors that his college internship had been falsified, that he was a drunk that was routinely seen in bars in St. Cloud, and that he had been sued for malpractice. It not only damaged his reputation, but his business suffered."

"All because Dad refused to redraw a few silly names," Francy shook her head and sighed. "It's entirely about politics."

Della's face went white. "Oh, dear. Now I know *why* they asked me to be the chairperson. I hope this doesn't do damage to Paul's reputation! What can I do?"

The group sat in silence, each one deep in thought.

"Why not let the Governor choose who he wants in the boat?" Lainey asked.

Francy rolled her eyes. "Absolutely not. He'd pick his cronies, for sure. The press would have a field day with that."

"I can see the headlines now," Vera winced. "Local Croaker's Wife Fills Governor's Boat With Hand-Picked Stink Bait."

Della shivered. "Good grief."

"Every entrant is assigned a number, correct? Well, since the purpose is to get free publicity for the Governor, why not hold a press conference and draw numbers, like a lottery," Lainey suggested.

"Hmm…" Francy said aloud. "That might work. People love lotteries. What do you think, Della?"

"If it means keeping Paul out of the line of fire, I'm all for it. I'll let the committee know tomorrow morning."

Vera sighed, clearly debating what she was about to say. "Why not hold the event at Backwater?"

The surprised look on Francy's face was unmistakable.

"Mom, why are you promoting Shep's place?"

"The committee is buying all the bait from Charlie this year."

"You told Shep, didn't you?" Francy said angrily. "You know that just stirs up more trouble between him and Charlie."

Vera rolled her eyes and frowned. "Yes, I told him. So have your little ticket drawing at his place. That'll even things up."

"Vera!" Della groaned. "I'll try to persuade the committee."

As hard as she tried, Lainey couldn't stop grinning or chuckling.

"Don't you laugh," Vera said. "Shep's just a crusty old…"

"Della, I think Mom and Lainey need to be on hand for the drawing, don't you?" Francy winked.

"Oh, you better believe it. I'm not walking the plank alone!"

"Hmpf!" Vera grunted, crossing her arms.

Click below for your copy today!

Murder in the Backwater

Christmas Corpse at Caribou Cabin Preview

Here's a sneak peak at Christmas Corpse at Caribou Cabin

The town of Mirror Falls had slipped into its annual pre-winter funk with the end of Daylight Savings Time and the inevitable long days of icy darkness that loomed ahead. Lainey was not looking forward to the dreary weeks with little to no sunshine. The thought of several feet of snow that would soon grace her yard and freeze into blackish piles as the winter progressed was a reminder for her to buy a new snow shovel.

    The year had been the busiest and most stressful one that Lainey could remember. The insurance company that employed her had been sold and the new owners increased her workload by at least half. Thanksgiving was a couple of days away and she had already put over 40,000 miles on her KIA, traveling to ten states for difficult fraud investigations. She was tired and looking for some downtime during the upcoming Christmas holiday.

Thankfully, the Whoopee group was meeting tonight for their Thanksgiving dinner and card games. Lainey was bringing her special cauliflower crusted veggie pizza and a Greek salad with her favorite roasted Mediterranean olives. She looked forward to sharing good food and forgetting about work for a short while. The group always met at 5:30 in the evening and took turns hosting. Tonight was Vera's turn.

As Lainey drove onto Vera's street, she noticed Shep's car parked in the driveway.

Hmm, Shep must be joining us. Sure hope he made that razzle-dazzle berry cobbler I love so much! Lainey thought to herself.

She parked her car on the street, got out and carried her dinner contributions to the front door. Before she could ring the doorbell, Francy opened the glass front door and welcomed her in with a huge smile.

"Yea! Lainey's here and she's brought the pizza!"

"Whoop, Whoop!" Della said as she walked from the kitchen to greet Lainey at the door. "I've been hungry for pizza all day. Come inside. I'll take your food to the table."

"Thanks, Della."

Lainey handed her the two containers of food and quickly took off her shoes and hung her coat in the small entryway closet. The townhome was an open concept design. Her front door opened to a large room that served as the living room, a small dining area, and the kitchen. The vaulted ceiling made the space seem much larger. Vera decorated for every season. Norwegian snowmen gnomes for January. Hearts and redbirds for Valentine's Day. Leprechauns and shamrocks for St. Patrick's Day. If it was a holiday, she had special decor to celebrate it.

Tonight was to celebrate Thanksgiving and Lainey expected to see the usual turkeys, horns of plenty, and pilgrim decorations. Instead, she saw black carved bear figurines and reindeer of all sizes placed around. Pillows on the living room couch were stitched with Welcome to the Cabin and Cabin Living is the Life.

As Lainey walked toward the kitchen, her skin tingled. She felt a familiar feeling of anxiousness in her stomach that forced her intuition into high gear. She'd felt this many times before and it always served as a warning that something unexpected was about to occur.

What in the world? Get a grip! She told herself silently. *This is just the Whoopee group, for Pete's sake. Vera decorated differently this year. What's the big deal?*

"Hurry up, Lainey. We're hungry and we don't want

the food to get cold," Shep said as he pulled out a dining room chair for Vera.

"I'm coming, I'm coming." Goosebumps covered her from head to toe and she knew her instincts were on point once again. She sat down across the table from Vera, not knowing that her holiday plans of rest and relaxation were about to change.

Vera Abernathy loved to entertain and had been doing so for almost half a century. She hosted the weekly coffee hour at the Mirror Falls Senior Center every Tuesday morning and brought treats and games to the YMCA's monthly Brunch with a Senior event. She was head of her church's funeral food committee and regularly took treats to the police station where Francy worked. Since she had been dating Shep Morton, the chef and owner of the Backwater Restaurant, she had recruited him to make the goodies she shared. It left her more time to decorate!

Tonight was no exception. A lush hunter green cloth covered the pedestal dining table and the dark color highlighted the crystal wine glasses that sat like royalty in front of each place setting. Vera hadn't used her Christmas Dickens' dishes, though. In their place were blue, speckled metal dinner plates and cups. There was a smorgasbord of food waiting to be devoured. Pickled beets, tater tot hot dish, veggie pizza, salad, pinto beans, and barbecued spare ribs filled the table.

"My goodness, Vera," Della smiled as she gazed at the steaming variety of food. "I think you've got everyone's favorite here tonight."

"Shep and I tried to do just that. He was kind enough to prepare the ribs and…"

"Kind enough? You, my dear, ordered me to make ribs for Francy and the tater tot hot dish for Della!" He raised his hand in a mock salute, then leaned toward her, putting his arm around her shoulders.

"Now, Shep, you just stop that. I did not order you," her tone was matter-of-fact, but lightened when he kissed her cheek. "Well, maybe I encouraged you a little bit."

Everyone chuckled. What followed were thirty minutes of laughing, eating, clinking of forks and knives scraping up delicious bites of food on the metal plates, and toasts to the hostess.

"I'm completely stuffed!" Lainey grunted, leaning back in her chair. "I don't think I could hold another bite."

Shep smiled, scooted his chair back and stood up. "That's too bad. I guess my razzle-dazzle berry cobbler with mocha ice cream will have to go into the trash bin."

"Don't you dare throw out one spoonful! I'll make room, even if it kills me!"

He laughed and turned to Vera. "Sweetie, would you help me dish up the dessert?"

"You know I have special bowls for the cobbler." She followed him into the kitchen.

Della, Francy, and Lainey looked at each other and spoke at the same time.

"What's going on with your Mom?" Lainey asked quietly.

"And what's with the chuck wagon dishes and wild animals everywhere?" Della added.

Francy shrugged her shoulders. "You know as much as I do. I've never seen these metal plates or decorations before. Who knows what these two are planning."

"Humph," Vera cleared her throat as she walked back to the table. She spoke like a mother scolding her child. "And what do you mean 'these two are planning', young lady?"

"Mom, I know you. You decorate with a theme in mind. And this is definitely not your favorite pilgrims on the Mayflower decorations."

"Shep and I have a little surprise for you ladies and it starts with dessert!" She handed a sealed envelope to each of them. "Don't open it until I tell you to."

Confusion and skepticism was apparent on the faces of the three friends. Della took hers and sniffed it, checking to see if it had perfume or a scent that might give an idea of what was inside. But there was nothing.

"Here's your winter wonderland vacation dessert,

ladies. Enjoy!" Shep said proudly as he presented the cobbler and ice cream.

Each serving was in a large white coffee mug. Around the top and bottom of each mug was a red plaid band. The words 'Welcome to Reindeer Lodge' were across the top band and the the words 'Hot Cocoa, Sleigh Rides, Fun' were written in the bottom band. The middle of the cup resembled an old, grayish wooden fence. A reindeer with large antlers stood in front of it.

"Wait a second," Francy began, "I've heard of Reindeer Lodge, but I can't remember why."

"Your dad and I spent our honeymoon there," Vera smiled. "Open your envelopes!"

Giggles, oohs, and ahs followed as the contents of the envelopes were revealed. Inside each was a photo of a very young Vera and Doc Abernathy hugging each other in front of the lodge. Also inside was a coupon for a free hot cocoa and a folded handwritten note which read 'You have my utmost thanks.' It was signed by Jim McAndrews.

"I love the photo, but who is Jim and why is he thanking us?" Lainey asked. Della and Francy nodded.

"Paul and I have friends who have gone to Reindeer Lodge for years for their family reunion," Della stated. "But since the pandemic hit a couple of years ago, they haven't been back. I didn't think it was still open."

"You've hit the nail on the head, Della," Vera answered. "Shep can fill you in better than I can."

"Eat your cobbler while it's still hot and I'll tell you the entire story," he said.

The ladies ate and Shep began explaining. He and Jim McAndrews served together in the 3rd Battalion, 325th Airborne Infantry at Fort Bragg, North Carolina.

"The 3rd of the 325th was assigned to the 82nd Airborne Division. Jim and I met during combat night jumps in 1973 and have remained friends since," Shep smiled. "He always thought his parachute wasn't going to open."

Everyone had finished their dessert and were listening intently to his story.

"Tell them how Jim married after the service, bought the Reindeer Lodge and has been running it all these years," Vera urged. "They want to hear about the vaca…"

"Mom, let him finish!" Francy rolled her eyes and sighed.

"She tells me to get to the point all the time," he took hold of Vera's hand and continued. "She's correct. Jim and his wife ran the lodge quite successfully. They had two boys and had made plans to retire one day, hoping one son would take it over."

He paused for a moment and his voice cracked when he spoke again. "But life doesn't go the way we plan. Vera and I have experienced that. Jim's wife died six years ago and since then, he's done the best he could."

The ladies listened while Shep explained that for the last three years, Jim had been struggling to make ends meet. He finally realized that his only option was to sell the lodge after the current Christmas season.

There was a subtle feeling of sadness as the five people sat silently, thinking about Jim and the lodge.

"What about his sons?" Lainey asked. "Would one of them buy it or run it?"

"I'm not sure of the details, but the older son is a financial advisor and has no desire to be involved with the lodge. The younger son works as his dad's general handyman-maintenance guy," Shep answered.

"Jim is the chef and has been doing the housekeeping duties since his wife passed," Vera shook her head. "It's my understanding that Kevin, the younger son, isn't a chef or interested in being a chef. It seems he doesn't have the finances to buy it either."

Della stood up and began clearing the table. "Okay. Francy and Lainey and I will clear the table so we can play cards. Shep, you and Vera stay seated and tell us why Jim is thanking us."

"Great idea," Francy said. "You two take turns or Mom, let Shep speak. Either way, spill the rest of the story!"

"Well, I see that the bossy gene definitely runs in the family!" Shep grinned.

"She does take after me, doesn't she?" Vera chided proudly. "That's the Abernathy women for you!"

The sadness in the air evaporated and the room filled with laughter once more.

"Last week, Jim called me…from the hospital. He was involved in a snowmobile accident," Shep said. "He suffered a broken arm, damaged rotator cuff, and a broken leg."

"He wants Shep to come to the lodge to cook and keep it running through the Christmas holidays," Vera chimed in. "And I'm going with him!"

"We want all of you to go with us," Shep added.

The ladies looked at each other in disbelief. Francy was the first to speak.

"A free Christmas vacation at a lodge in northern Minnesota? I'm in!"

"Count me in, too!" Della replied.

"That's just what I have been needing. A vacation with Shep's food and hot cocoa!" Lainey exclaimed. "I'd go today if I could."

Shep and Vera looked at each other hesitantly.

"We'd like you to drive up with us the day after Thanksgiving," Vera said sheepishly.

The goosebumps Lainey first felt had gone away once she sat down to eat. But now, they were back and she felt a little nauseous.

"Wait a second, what else are you not telling us?" she questioned. "There's more to this, isn't there."

It was Vera who rolled her eyes this time.

"Shep and I drove to the Rainy Lake Medical Center in International Falls to see Jim last weekend. His son Kevin was there and he took us to the lodge after our visit."

"The lodge needs work and…" Shep paused. "It needs a very thorough cleaning."

"I've never seen so many dust bunnies in corners in my life!" Vera frowned and shivered. "I despise those darn things!"

Della crossed her arms and looked at Francy. One side of Francy's mouth was turned up in a snarl. Lainey nodded her head slowly.

"And that is why the cabin-looking decorations and our favorite dishes tonight. Bribery at its best!" she winked at Shep.

"Let me get this straight," Della began. "A free vacation – if we become the Whoopee Merry Maids Cleaning Service, correct?"

"Well…" Vera started to speak.

"Don't try to deny it, Mom," Francy kidded.

Shep gave a big belly laugh. "Yep! It was all Vera's idea!"

"Why you old goat!" She pretended to be offended, but then grinned. "The cleaning crew *was* my idea, but *you* bought the mugs!"

"Okay, okay," Lainey laughed. "Is there internet service at the Lodge? I do have vacation time, but I will need to do some work if we are planning on staying a couple of weeks."

Once again Vera looked at Shep and shrugged her shoulders. "You wanna answer that?"

"Yes, but both cell and internet service can be spotty. If you have work or need better service, Ranier or International Falls are only a few miles away. I'm sure either town will have a coffee shop or two." He paused to gage their reactions before continuing carefully.

"Actually, we need you to stay until after Christmas. Della could bring Paul and Francy could bring Roger. Wouldn't that..."

"Hold on," Francy interrupted, raising her hand. "Stay for a month? Bring Roger and Paul?" She crossed her arms and leaned back her chair.

"Something sounds very fishy to me," Della replied, leaning forward, clasping her hands together, placing them on the table in front or her. "In fact, it smells as bad as Shep's stink bait concoction."

"I hear ice fishing is great up there," Vera chimed in with a forced chuckle, hoping to smooth over the questions she knew were coming next.

Lainey sat quietly, listening and watching Shep and Vera's body language. She took in a deep breath and blew it out, shaking her head as if to wake herself up. Then she spoke.

"It seems we're to be the housekeeping staff for the

holidays," pointing her finger at the two sitting across from her. "You two think you're pretty sneaky, don't you?"

"I know it's a lot to ask," Shep began as his voiced cracked once more. "It's just that Jim's finances are gone and selling this lodge is his last resort to avoid bankruptcy or foreclosure. We…" his eyes teared up and he had to stop for a moment before going on. "We are his only hope."

Della, Francy, and Lainey glanced at each other and without hesitation agreed.

"Thank you, girls," Shep replied.

"Your smile is enough thanks for us," Della said.

"Now do you girls see why I let this old goat be my boyfriend? He has a heart of gold!" Vera announced proudly.

"And he's a great cook, too!" Francy teased.

"Well, there is that," Vera grinned.

"Enough of the flattery…you're making this old man blush! I'll make sure you are all fed very well! Now, are we going to play cards or not?" Shep laughed.

About the Author

Laura Hern is an author who writes Cozy Mysteries and Romance novels.

She loves cats, charred brussel sprouts with bacon, and romantic murder mysteries!

Laura grew up in Texas and lives in Minnesota. She loves to ride motorcycles, and is an avid domino and card player. Music and traveling are her passions.

Follow me on Facebook, Amazon, and Twitter!

Also by Laura Hern

Lainey Maynard Mystery Series:

The Family Tree Murders

Murder In the BackWater

Curtain Call At Brooksey's Playhouse

Christmas Corpse at Caribou Cabin

Roommates

The Pew Maker

Always Be My Love

And many more to come soon!

Made in the USA
Middletown, DE
28 November 2023